SKYWALKER STRIKES: VOLUME 1

It is a period of renewed hope for the Rebellion.

The evil Galactic Empire's greatest weapon, the Death Star, has been destroyed by the young Rebel pilot, Luke Skywalker.

With the Imperial Forces in disarray, the Rebels look to press their advantage by unleashing a daring offensive throughout the far reaches of space, hoping to defeat the Empire once and for all and at last restore freedom to the galaxy....

JASON AARON
Writer

JOHN CASSADAY
Artist

LAURA MARTIN
Colorist

CHRIS ELIOPOULOS
Letterer

CASSADAY & MARTIN
Cover Artists

CHARLES BEACHAM
Assistant Editor

JORDAN D. WHITE
Editor

C.B. CEBULSKI &
MIKE MARTS
Executive Editors

AXEL
ALONSO
Editor In Chief

JOE
QUESADA
Chief Creative Officer

DAN
BUCKLEY
Publisher

For Lucasfilm:
Senior Editor JENNIFER HEDDLE
Lucasfilm Story Group RAYNE ROBERTS, PABLO HIDALGO,
LELAND CHEE

ABDO
Spotlight

ABDOPUBLISHING.COM

Reinforced library bound edition published in 2017 by Spotlight,
a division of ABDO, PO Box 398166, Minneapolis, Minnesota 55439.
Spotlight produces high-quality reinforced library bound editions for
schools and libraries. Published by agreement with Marvel Characters, Inc.

Printed in the United States of America, North Mankato, Minnesota.
042016
092016

THIS BOOK CONTAINS
RECYCLED MATERIALS

marvelkids.com

PUBLISHER'S CATALOGING IN PUBLICATION DATA

Names: Aaron, Jason, author. | Cassaday, John ; Martin, Laura, illustrators.
Title: Star Wars : Skywalker strikes / by Jason Aaron ; illustrated by Laura Martin
   and John Cassaday.
Description: Minneapolis, MN : Spotlight, [2017] | Series: Star Wars : Skywalker
   strikes
Summary: Luke Skywalker and the ragtag rebels opposing the Galactic Empire are
   fresh off their biggest victory so far-the destruction of the massive Death Star!
   But the Empire's not toppled yet! Join Luke, Princess Leia, Han Solo,
   Chewbacca, C-3PO, R2-D2, and the rest of the Rebel Alliance as they fight for
   freedom against Darth Vader and his evil master, the Emperor!
Identifiers: LCCN 2016932364 | ISBN 9781614795278 (v.1 : lib. bdg.) | ISBN
   9781614795285 (v.2 : lib. bdg.) | ISBN 9781614795292 (v.3 : lib. bdg.) | ISBN
   9781614795308 (v.4 : lib. bdg.) | ISBN 9781614795315 (v.5 : lib. bdg.) | ISBN
   9781614795322 (v.6 : lib. bdg.)
Subjects: LCSH: Skywalker, Luke (Fictitious character)--Juvenile fiction. | Star Wars
   fiction--Comic books, strips, etc.--Juvenile fiction. | Graphic novels--Juvenile
   fiction.
Classification: DDC 741.5--dc23
LC record available at http://lccn.loc.gov/2016932364

Spotlight

A Division of ABDO

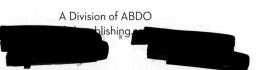

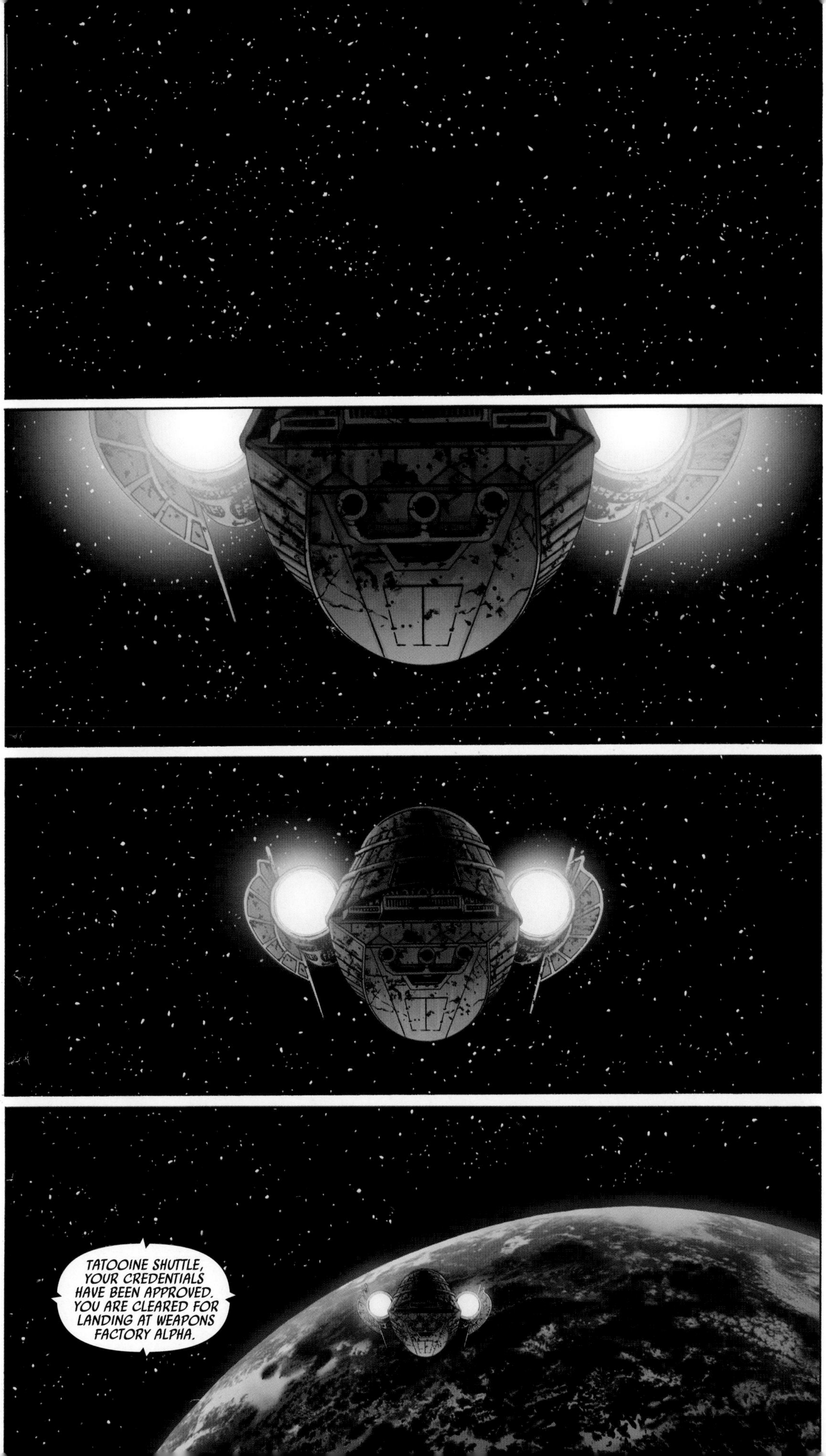
TATOOINE SHUTTLE, YOUR CREDENTIALS HAVE BEEN APPROVED. YOU ARE CLEARED FOR LANDING AT WEAPONS FACTORY ALPHA.

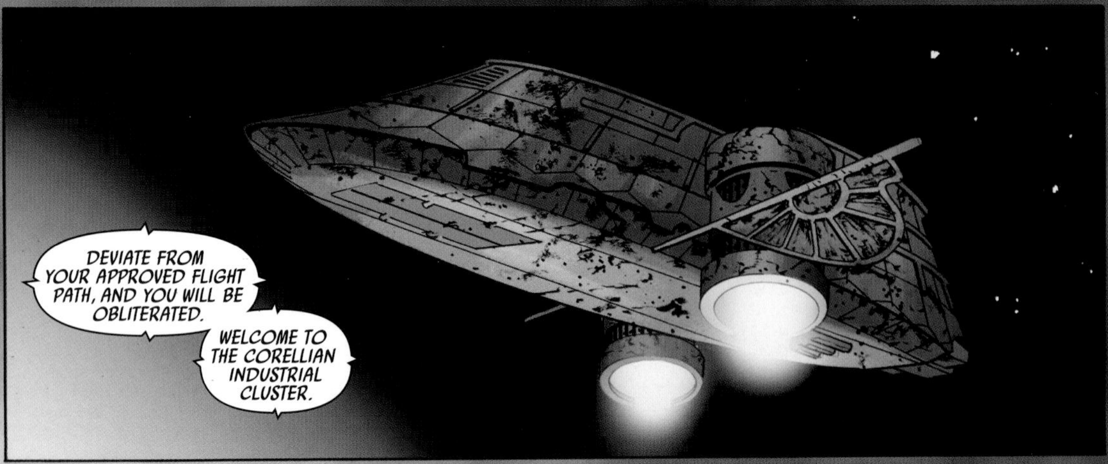
DEVIATE FROM YOUR APPROVED FLIGHT PATH, AND YOU WILL BE OBLITERATED.
WELCOME TO THE CORELLIAN INDUSTRIAL CLUSTER.

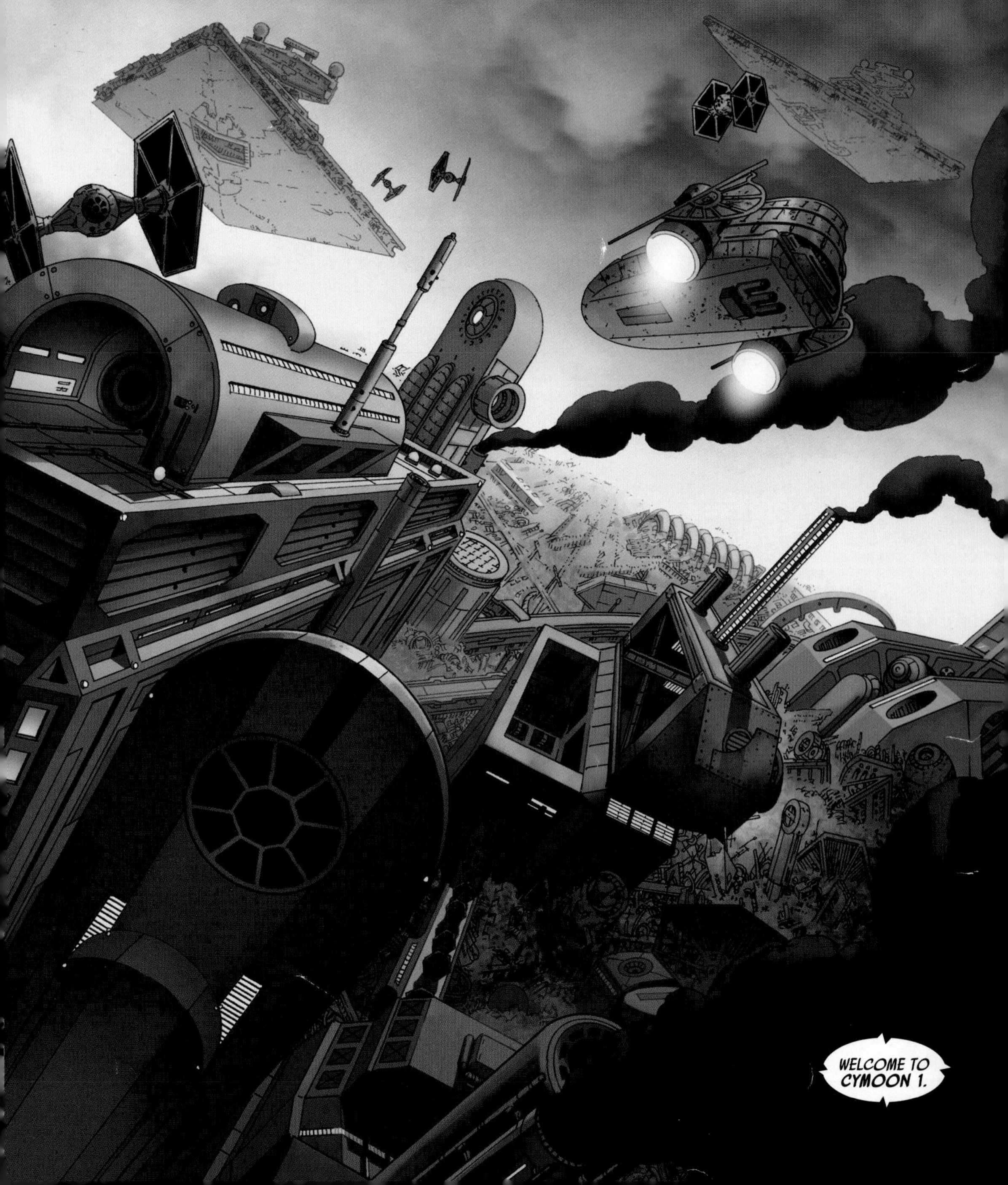
WELCOME TO CYMOON 1.

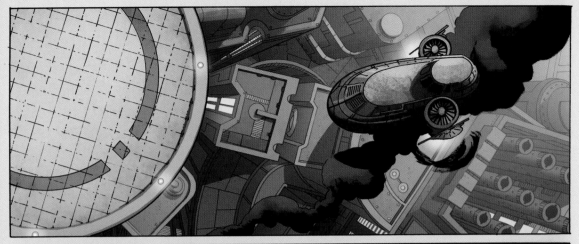

OUTER RIM SCUM. I CAN *SMELL* THEM ALREADY.

BE ON THE ALERT. IF ANYTHING SEEMS EVEN *REMOTELY* SUSPICIOUS...

...KILL THEM ALL.

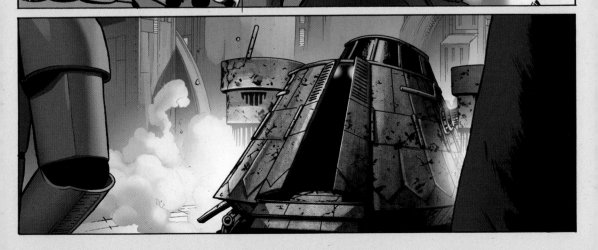

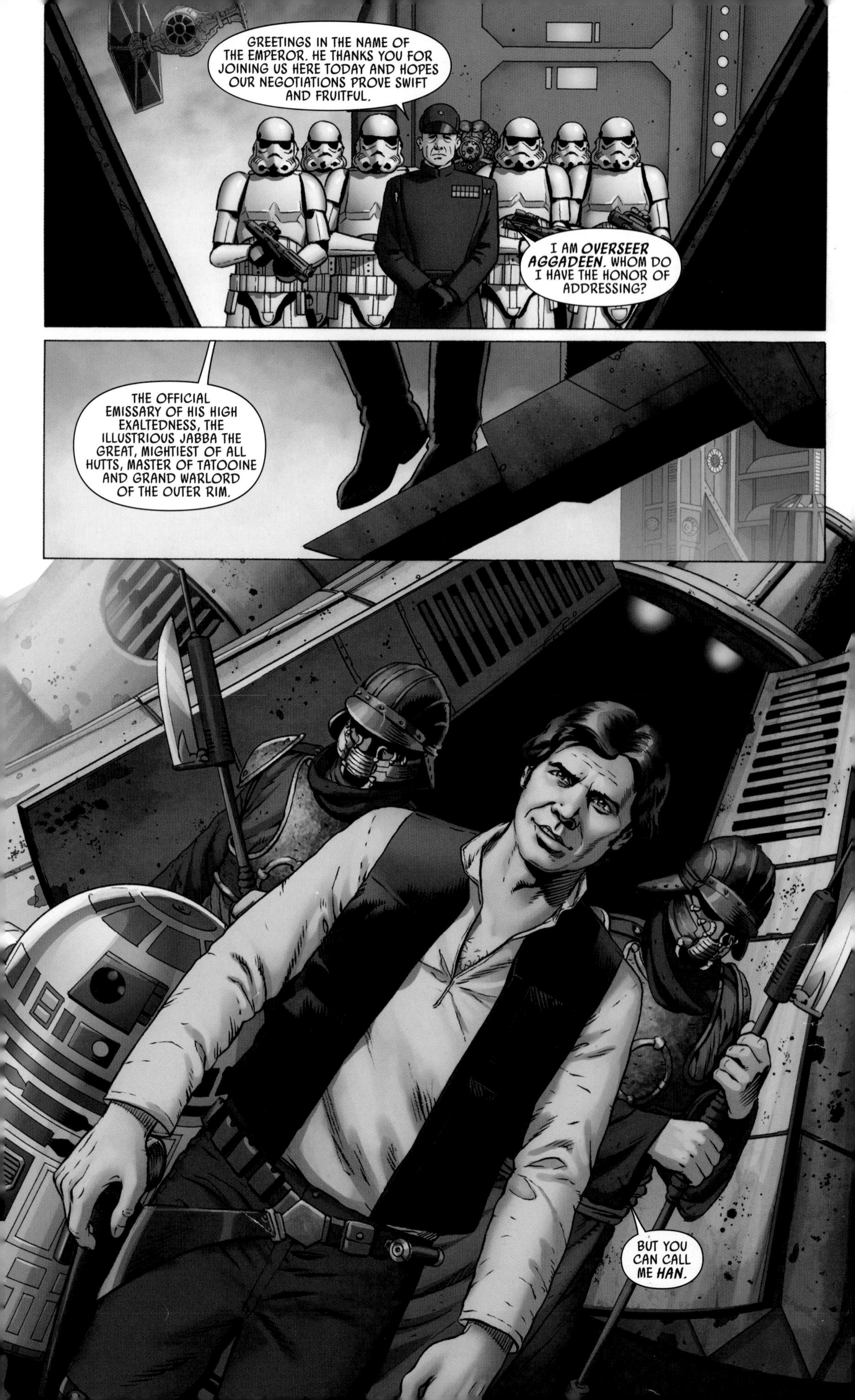
GREETINGS IN THE NAME OF THE EMPEROR. HE THANKS YOU FOR JOINING US HERE TODAY AND HOPES OUR NEGOTIATIONS PROVE SWIFT AND FRUITFUL.
I AM OVERSEER AGGADEEN. WHOM DO I HAVE THE HONOR OF ADDRESSING?
THE OFFICIAL EMISSARY OF HIS HIGH EXALTEDNESS, THE ILLUSTRIOUS JABBA THE GREAT, MIGHTIEST OF ALL HUTTS, MASTER OF TATOOINE AND GRAND WARLORD OF THE OUTER RIM.
BUT YOU CAN CALL ME HAN.

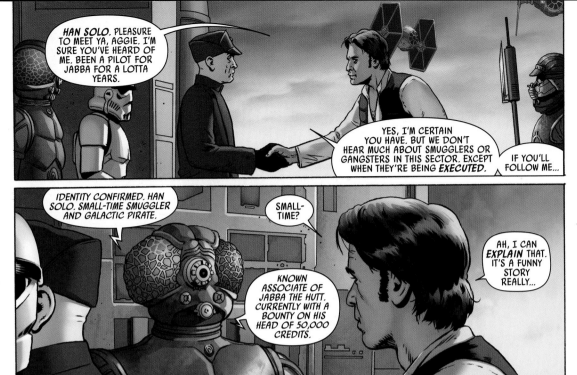

HAN SOLO. PLEASURE TO MEET YA, AGGIE. I'M SURE YOU'VE HEARD OF ME. BEEN A PILOT FOR JABBA FOR A LOTTA YEARS.

YES, I'M CERTAIN YOU HAVE. BUT WE DON'T HEAR MUCH ABOUT SMUGGLERS OR GANGSTERS IN THIS SECTOR. EXCEPT WHEN THEY'RE BEING *EXECUTED*.

IF YOU'LL FOLLOW ME...

IDENTITY CONFIRMED. HAN SOLO. SMALL-TIME SMUGGLER AND GALACTIC PIRATE.

SMALL-TIME?

KNOWN ASSOCIATE OF JABBA THE HUTT. CURRENTLY WITH A BOUNTY ON HIS HEAD OF 50,000 CREDITS.

AH, I CAN *EXPLAIN* THAT. IT'S A FUNNY STORY REALLY...

SOME OTHER TIME PERHAPS. YOUR... "BODYGUARDS" MUST LEAVE THEIR WEAPONS HERE. YOU WILL ALL BE SCANNED FOR BLASTERS.

IF YOU HAVE HIDDEN ONES, BEST TO TURN THEM OVER FREELY. WE WOULDN'T WANT TO START THE NEGOTIATIONS ON A SOUR NOTE, NOW WOULD WE?

NO, WE WOULDN'T WANT THAT.

YOU HEARD THE MAN, BODYGUARDS.

NO GUNS.

WE'RE GOING IN, EVERYONE, HOLD YOUR POSITIONS.

OH, THANK THE MAKER. I WAS HALF EXPECTING THEY WOULD KILL YOU ALL ON SIGHT.

THE SUBTERFUGE MUST ACTUALLY BE WORKING. THEY BELIEVE YOU TRULY **ARE** THE ENVOY FROM JABBA. WHEN OF COURSE THE **REAL** ENVOY WAS INTERCEPTED DAYS AGO BY THE REBEL FLEET.

THREEPIO... SHUT UP.

YES, OF COURSE, I'M JUST THRILLED TO SEE US FINALLY OPERATING LIKE A SUFFICIENTLY LUBRICATED MACHINE. IT WOULD SEEM THE TIDE OF WAR HAS FINALLY TURNED IN OUR FAVOR. IN SHORT, I DARE SAY...

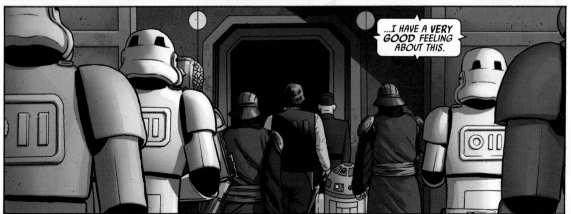

...I HAVE A **VERY** GOOD FEELING ABOUT THIS.

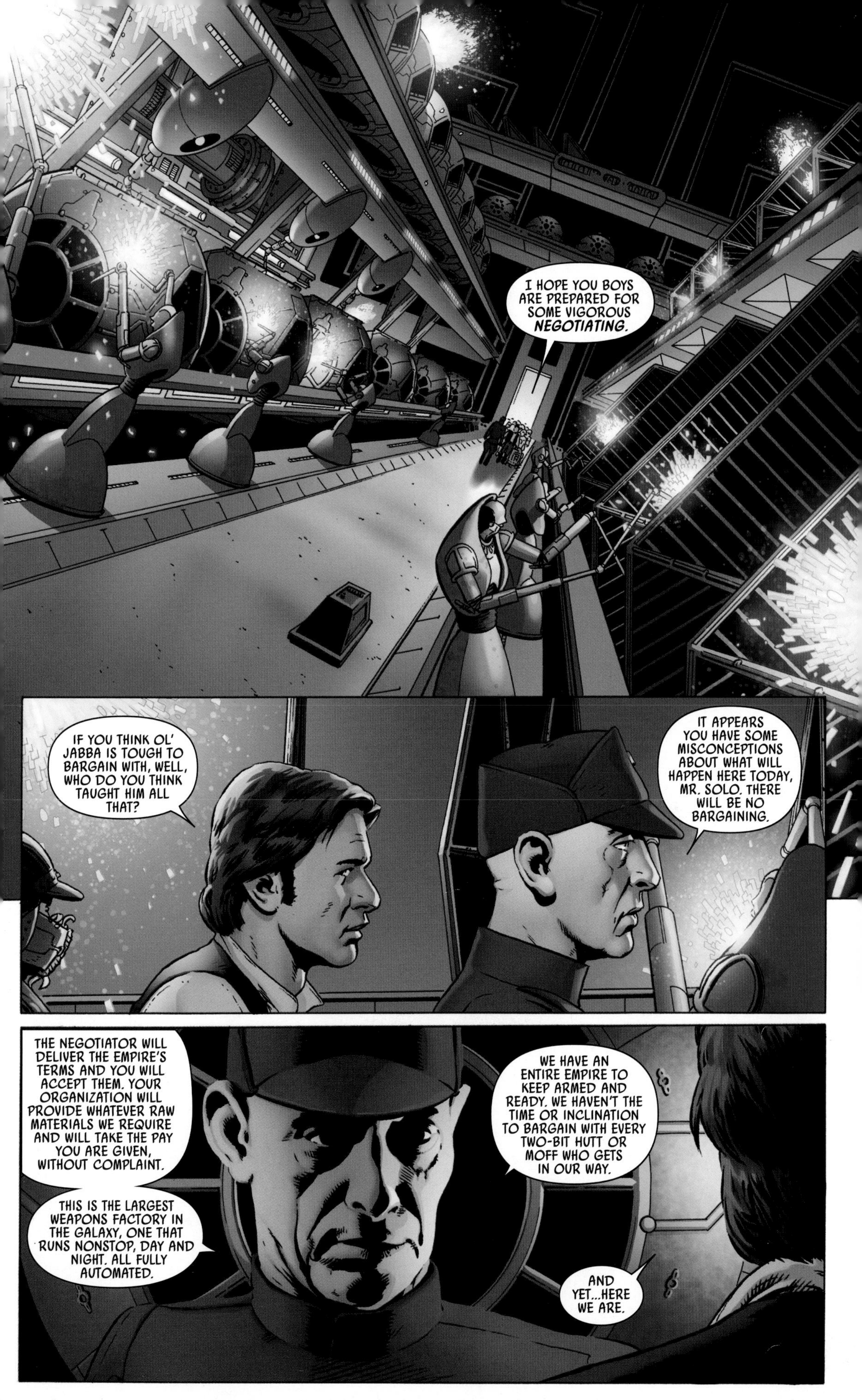
I HOPE YOU BOYS ARE PREPARED FOR SOME VIGOROUS NEGOTIATING.
IF YOU THINK OL' JABBA IS TOUGH TO BARGAIN WITH, WELL, WHO DO YOU THINK TAUGHT HIM ALL THAT?
IT APPEARS YOU HAVE SOME MISCONCEPTIONS ABOUT WHAT WILL HAPPEN HERE TODAY, MR. SOLO. THERE WILL BE NO BARGAINING.
THE NEGOTIATOR WILL DELIVER THE EMPIRE'S TERMS AND YOU WILL ACCEPT THEM. YOUR ORGANIZATION WILL PROVIDE WHATEVER RAW MATERIALS WE REQUIRE AND WILL TAKE THE PAY YOU ARE GIVEN, WITHOUT COMPLAINT.
THIS IS THE LARGEST WEAPONS FACTORY IN THE GALAXY, ONE THAT RUNS NONSTOP, DAY AND NIGHT. ALL FULLY AUTOMATED.
WE HAVE AN ENTIRE EMPIRE TO KEEP ARMED AND READY. WE HAVEN'T THE TIME OR INCLINATION TO BARGAIN WITH EVERY TWO-BIT HUTT OR MOFF WHO GETS IN OUR WAY.
AND YET...HERE WE ARE.

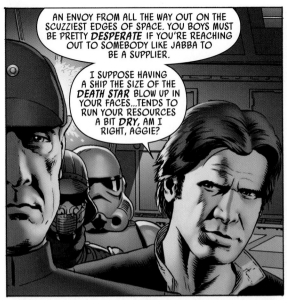

AN ENVOY FROM ALL THE WAY OUT ON THE SCUZZIEST EDGES OF SPACE. YOU BOYS MUST BE PRETTY *DESPERATE* IF YOU'RE REACHING OUT TO SOMEBODY LIKE JABBA TO BE A SUPPLIER.

I SUPPOSE HAVING A SHIP THE SIZE OF THE *DEATH STAR* BLOW UP IN YOUR FACES...TENDS TO RUN YOUR RESOURCES A BIT *DRY,* AM I RIGHT, AGGIE?

THE NEGOTIATOR WILL ARRIVE SHORTLY.

YOU WILL AWAIT HIM WITHIN.

I BET IT'S NICE AND QUIET IN THERE.

IT IS SHIELDED, YES.

YOU KNOW, I KINDA PREFER IT OUT HERE WHERE IT'S ALL LOUD AND NOISY.

DON'T BE IDIOTIC, WHY IN THE WORLD WOULD WE HOLD NEGOTIATIONS ON THE FACTORY FLOOR?

DON'T YOU REMEMBER? YOU SAID IT YOURSELF...

WE AREN'T HERE TO NEGOTIATE.

ARTOO...

YOUR DROID APPEARS TO BE LEAKING FLUIDS.

UM... ARTOO?

KZZZT

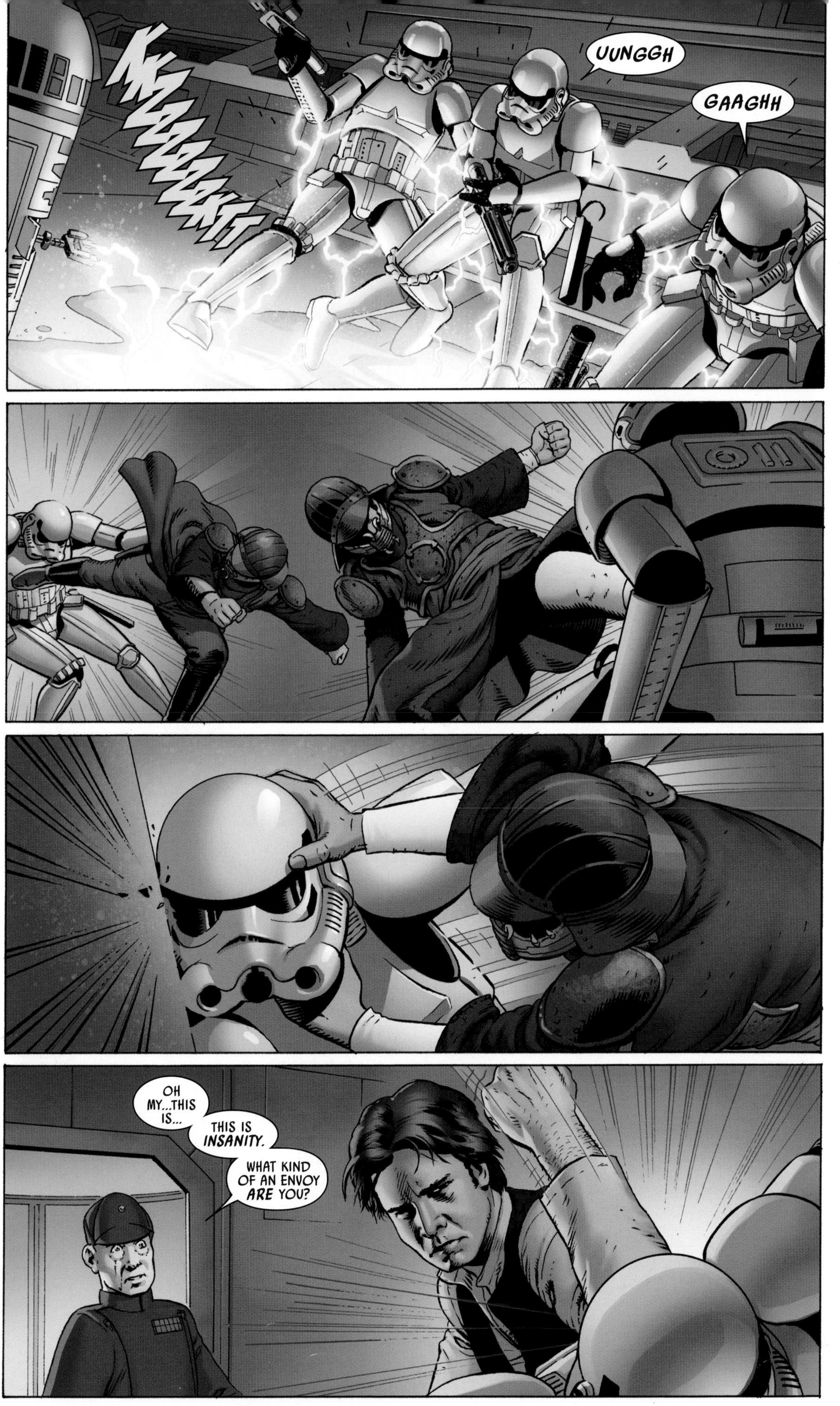
KKZZZZZKTT
UUNGGH
GAAGHH
OH MY...THIS IS...
THIS IS INSANITY.
WHAT KIND OF AN ENVOY ARE YOU?

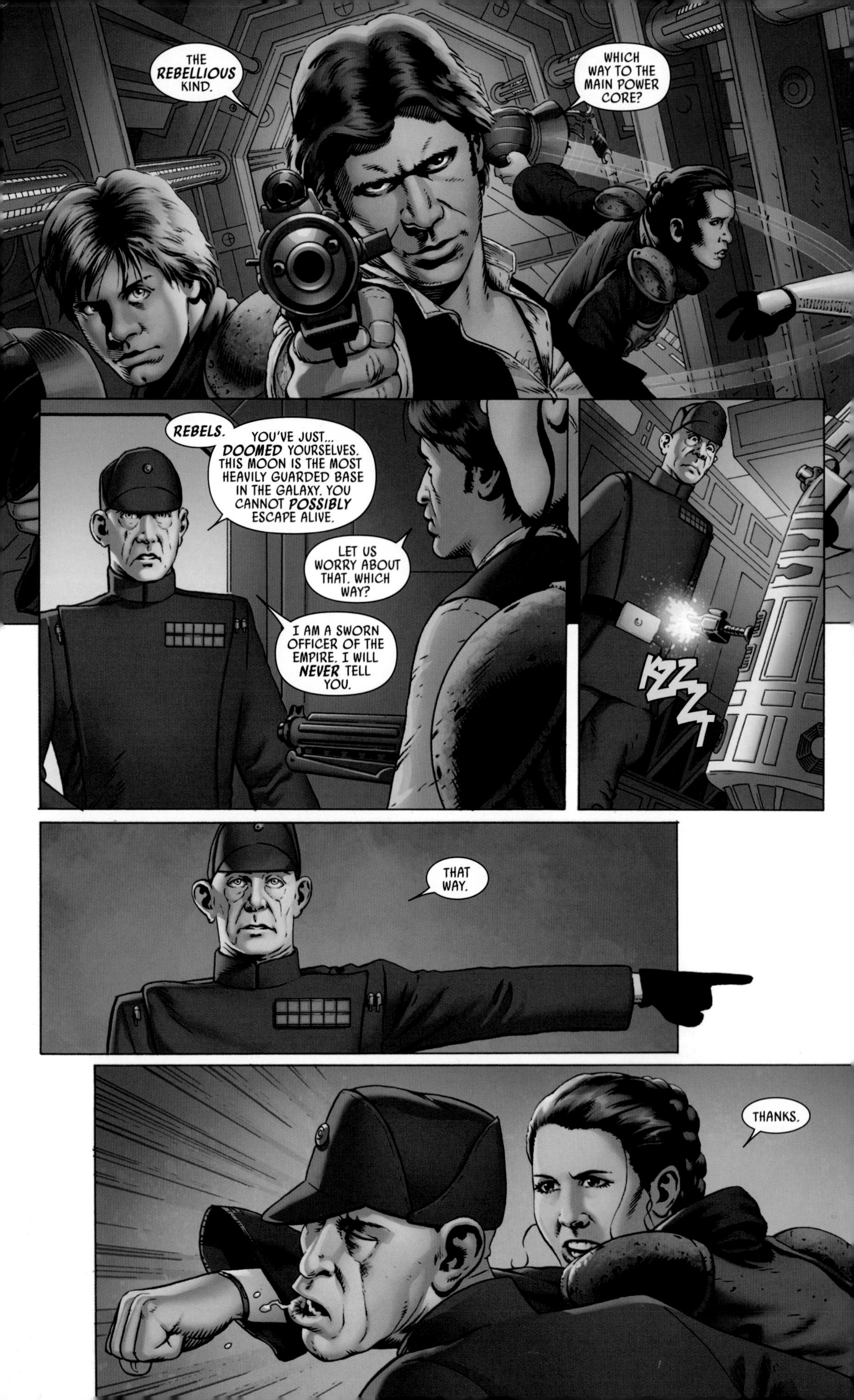
THE REBELLIOUS KIND.
WHICH WAY TO THE MAIN POWER CORE?
REBELS.
YOU'VE JUST... DOOMED YOURSELVES. THIS MOON IS THE MOST HEAVILY GUARDED BASE IN THE GALAXY. YOU CANNOT POSSIBLY ESCAPE ALIVE.
LET US WORRY ABOUT THAT. WHICH WAY?
I AM A SWORN OFFICER OF THE EMPIRE. I WILL NEVER TELL YOU.
KZZZT
THAT WAY.
THANKS.

NICE WORK, ARTOO.

WRRRRRRP BEEP BEEP

WE'RE IN. MOVE TO PHASE TWO.

THREEPIO, YOU WORTHLESS RUST BUCKET, YOU BETTER NOT HAVE DAMAGED MY SHIP.

FOR ONCE, SIR, THE MILLENNIUM FALCON ACTUALLY APPEARS TO BE IN GOOD WORKING ORDER.

AS WE HOPED, CHEWBACCA WAS ABLE TO PILOT US UNDETECTED THROUGH THE MOON'S ORBITAL DEBRIS FIELD.

AT PRESENT, THE FALCON AND I ARE SAFELY HIDDEN AMONGST THE RATHER EXTENSIVE REFUSE FIELDS THAT SURROUND THE FACTORY.

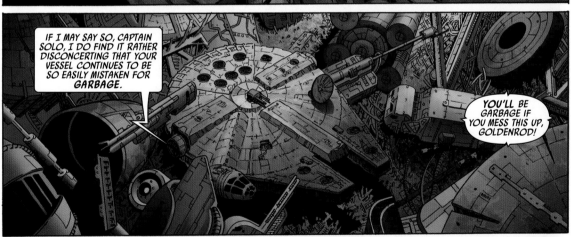

IF I MAY SAY SO, CAPTAIN SOLO, I DO FIND IT RATHER DISCONCERTING THAT YOUR VESSEL CONTINUES TO BE SO EASILY MISTAKEN FOR GARBAGE.

YOU'LL BE GARBAGE IF YOU MESS THIS UP, GOLDENROD!

THERE ARE AUTOMATED SENTRIES PATROLLING THIS AREA. I AM NOT CERTAIN HOW MUCH LONGER I CAN REMAIN UNDETECTED. I SUGGEST YOU ACT QUICKLY.

JUST BE READY TO HIT THE AUTO-PILOT AS SOON AS WE GIVE YOU THE SIGNAL.

YES, SIR. OF COURSE, SIR.

MAY THE FORCE BE WITH YOU, SIR.

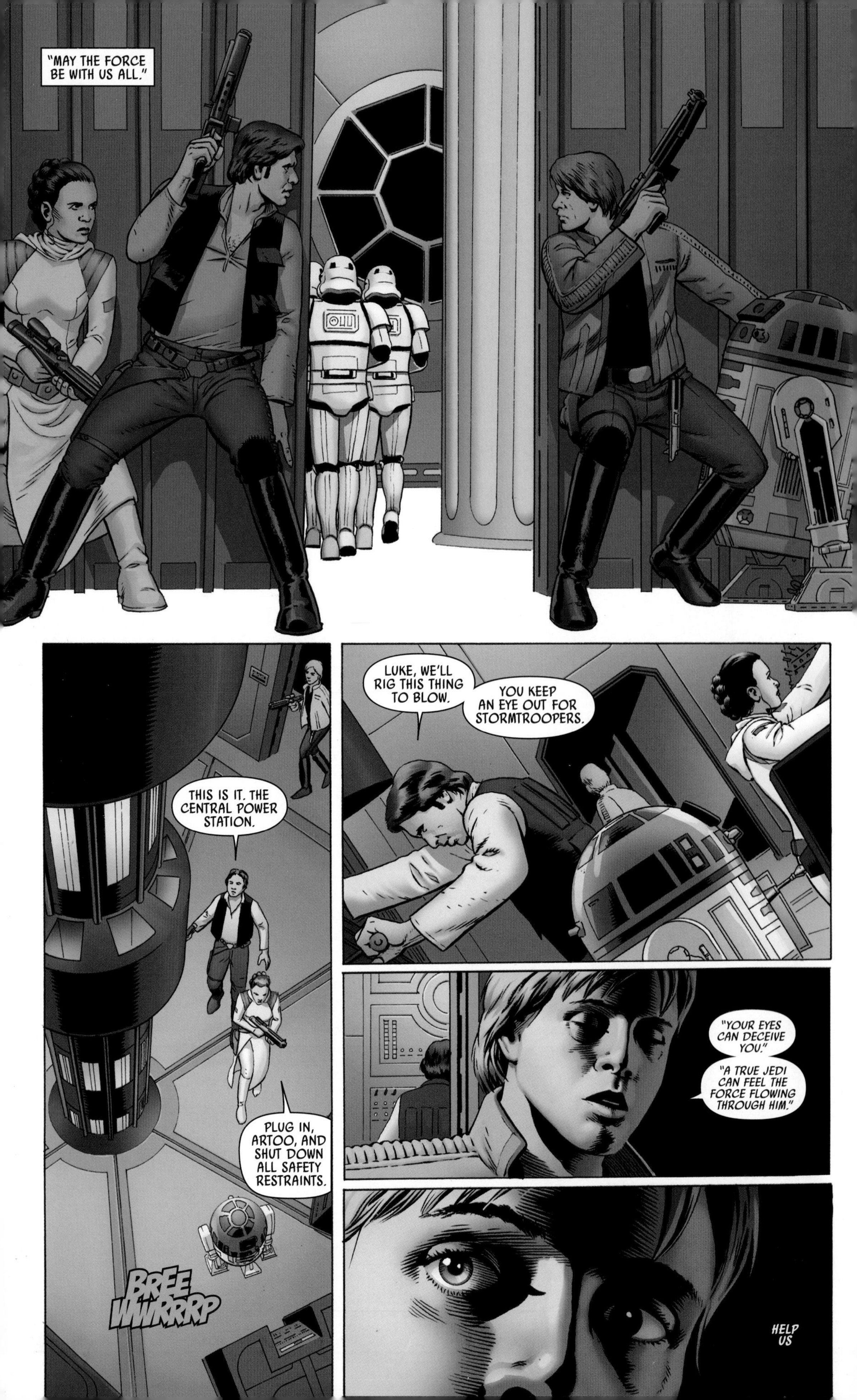
"MAY THE FORCE BE WITH US ALL."
THIS IS IT. THE CENTRAL POWER STATION.
PLUG IN, ARTOO, AND SHUT DOWN ALL SAFETY RESTRAINTS.
BREE WWRRRP
LUKE, WE'LL RIG THIS THING TO BLOW.
YOU KEEP AN EYE OUT FOR STORMTROOPERS.
"YOUR EYES CAN DECEIVE YOU."
"A TRUE JEDI CAN FEEL THE FORCE FLOWING THROUGH HIM."
HELP US

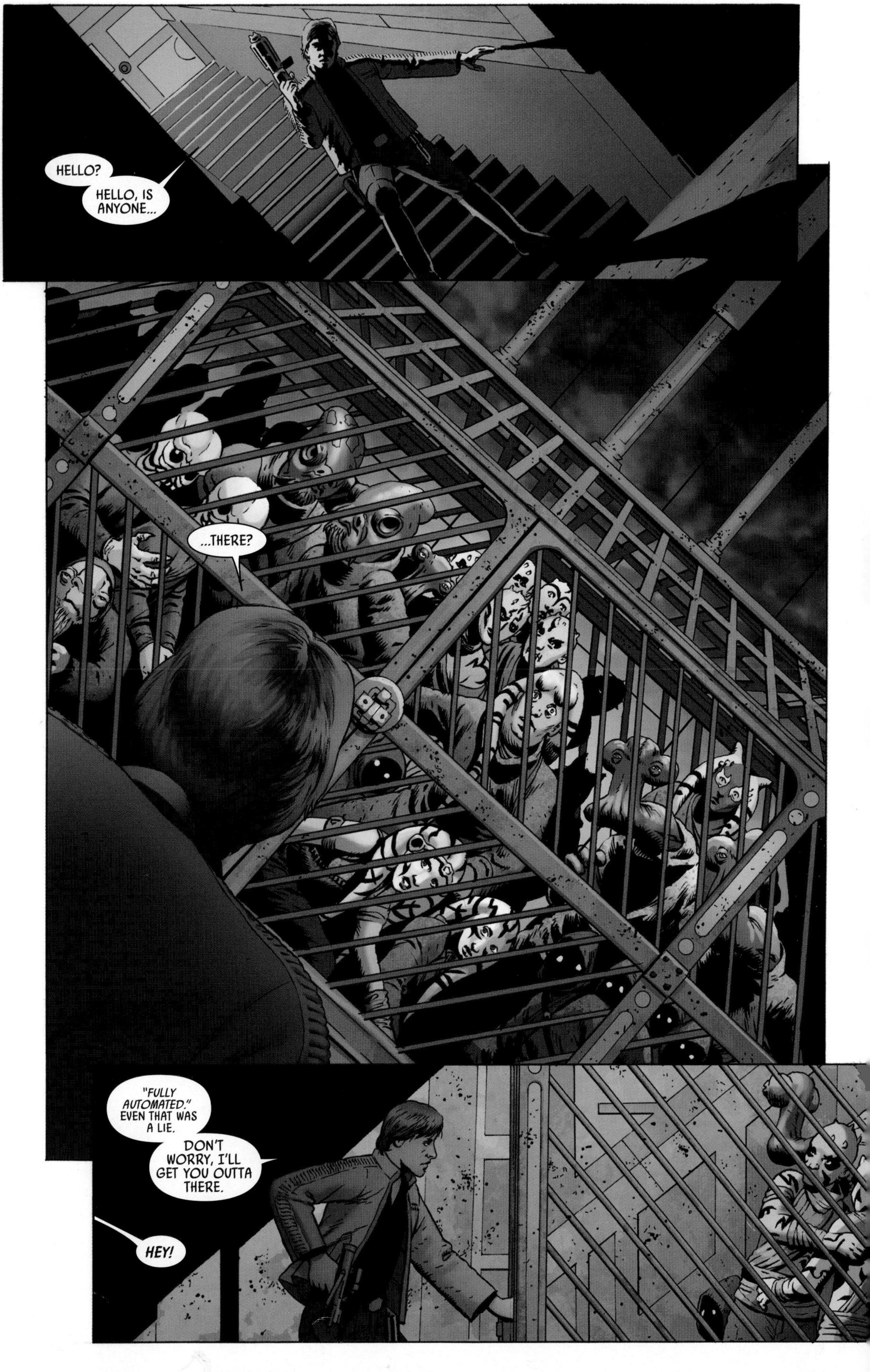
HELLO?
HELLO, IS ANYONE...
...THERE?
"FULLY AUTOMATED." EVEN THAT WAS A LIE.
DON'T WORRY, I'LL GET YOU OUTTA THERE.
HEY!

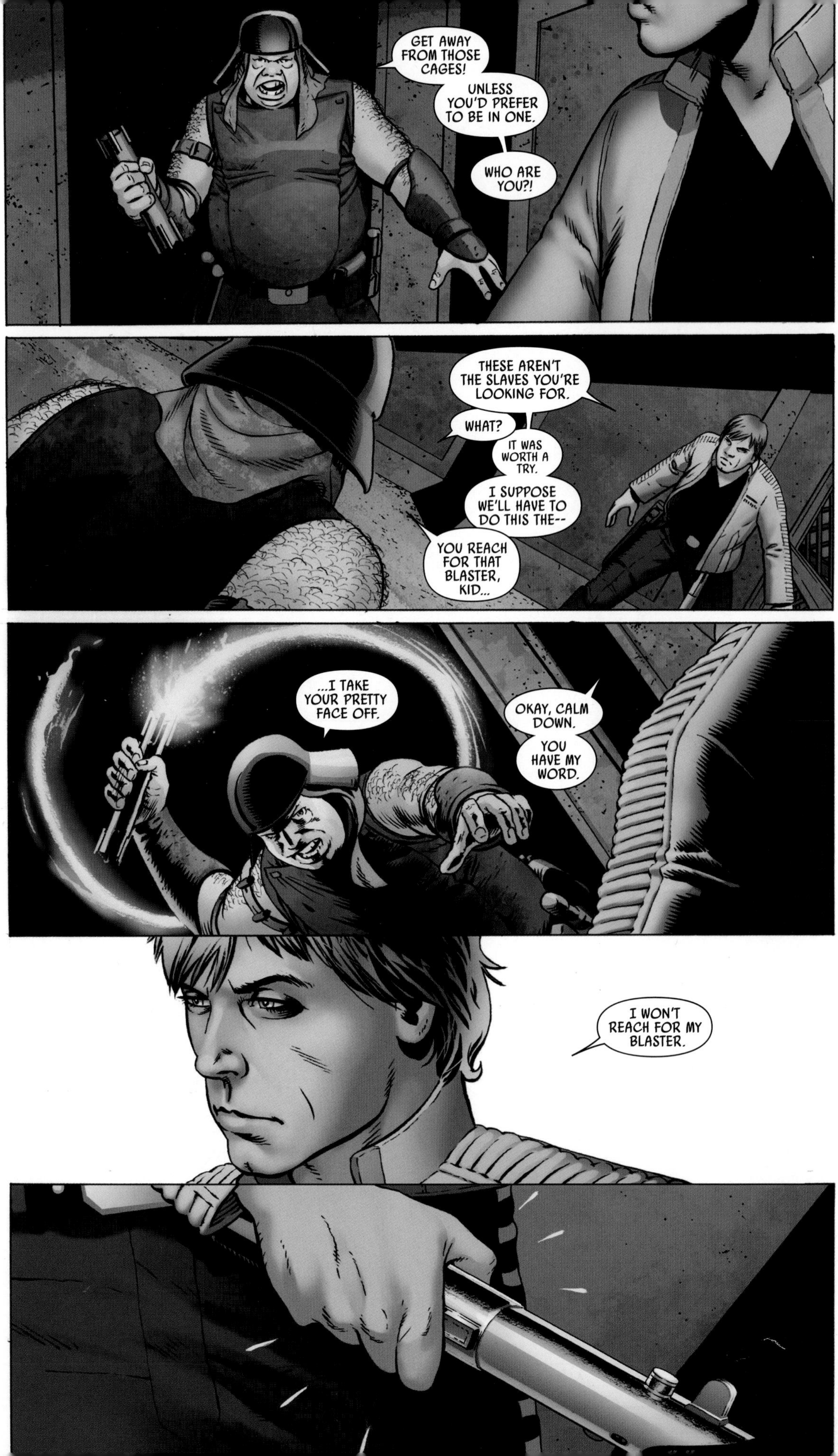
GET AWAY FROM THOSE CAGES!
UNLESS YOU'D PREFER TO BE IN ONE.
WHO ARE YOU?!
THESE AREN'T THE SLAVES YOU'RE LOOKING FOR.
WHAT?
IT WAS WORTH A TRY.
I SUPPOSE WE'LL HAVE TO DO THIS THE--
YOU REACH FOR THAT BLASTER, KID...
...I TAKE YOUR PRETTY FACE OFF.
OKAY, CALM DOWN.
YOU HAVE MY WORD.
I WON'T REACH FOR MY BLASTER.

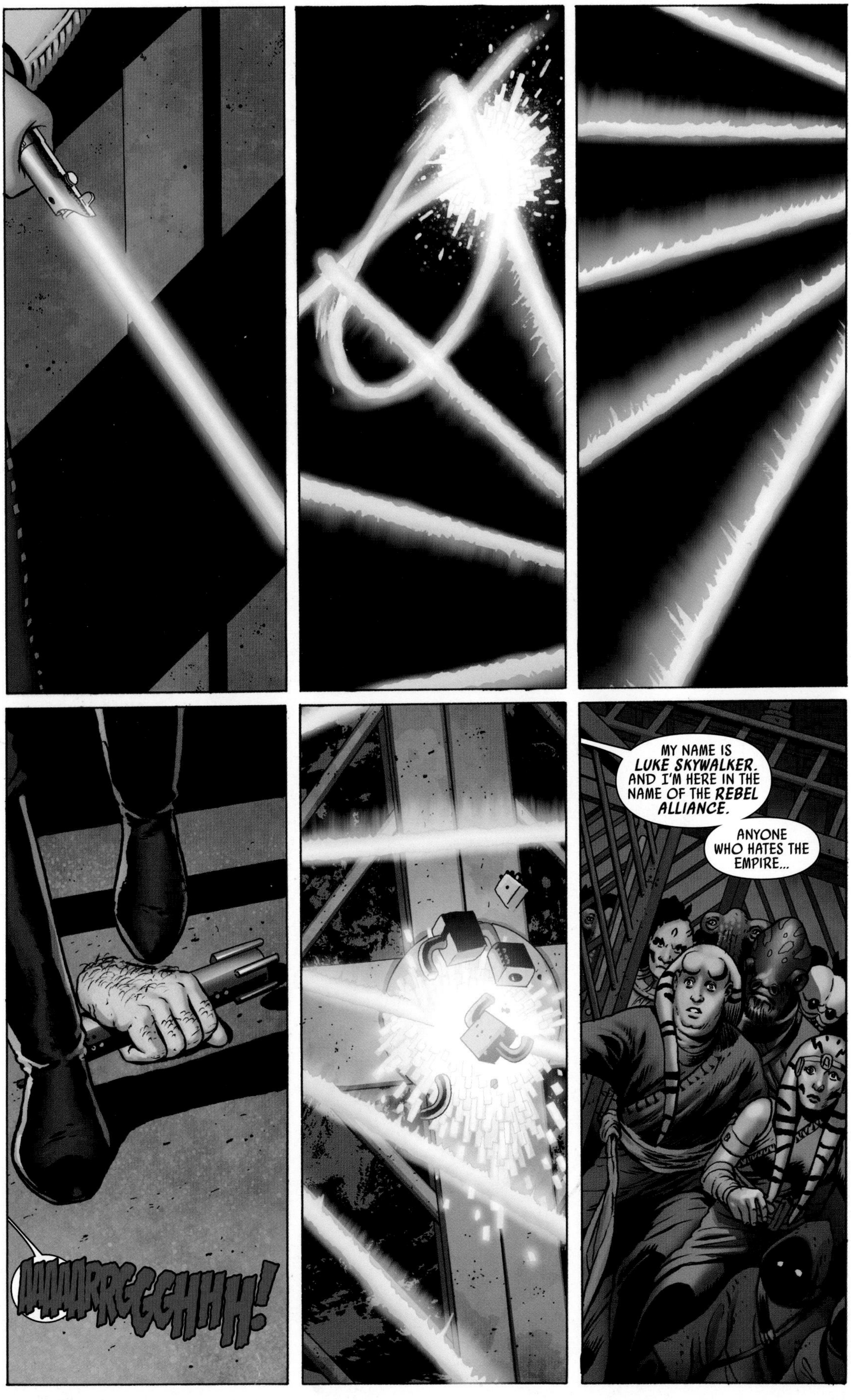
AAAAARRGGGHHHH!
MY NAME IS LUKE SKYWALKER. AND I'M HERE IN THE NAME OF THE REBEL ALLIANCE.
ANYONE WHO HATES THE EMPIRE...

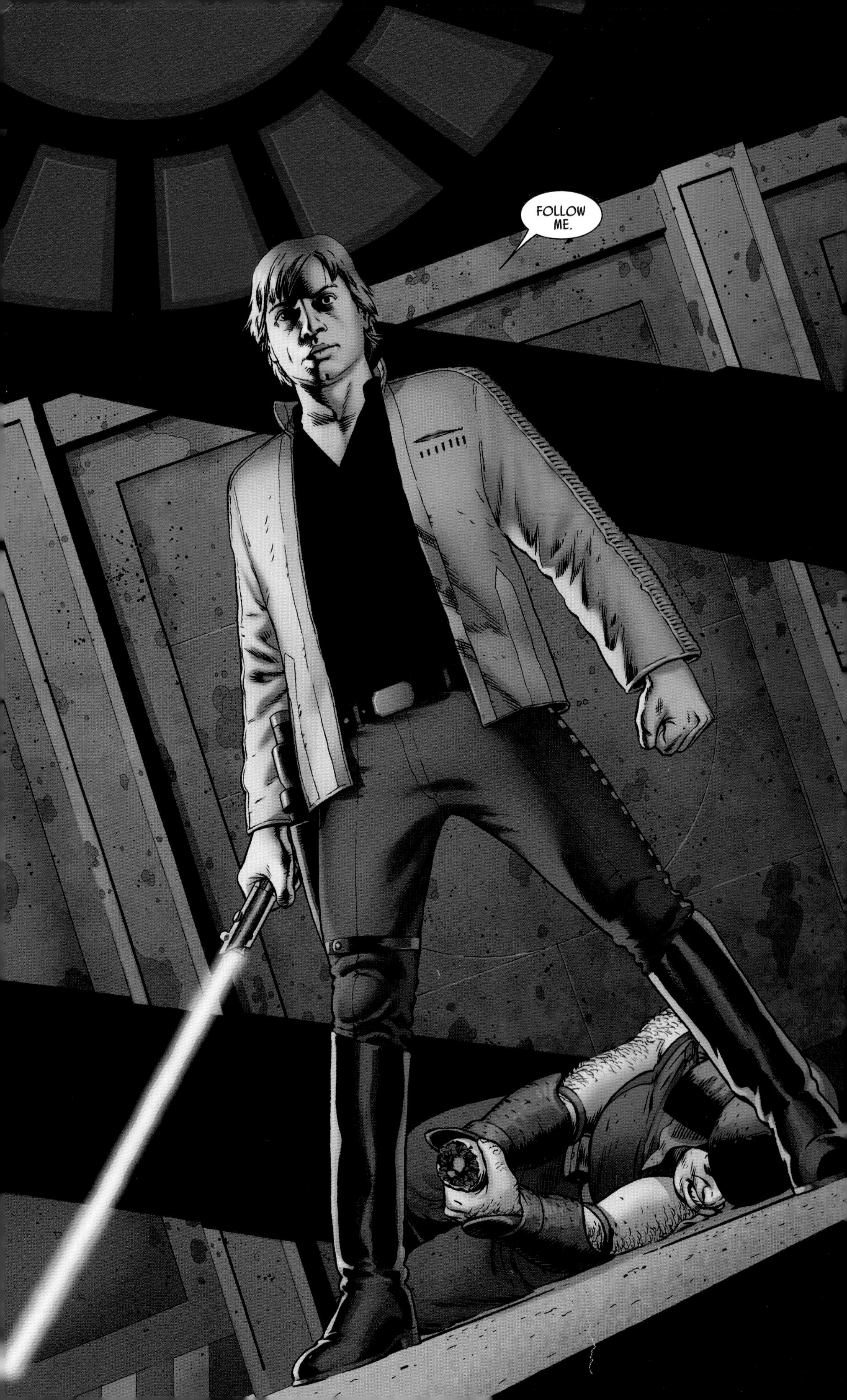
FOLLOW ME.

WHEEOOOO

COUNTDOWN'S STARTED. TEN MINUTES TO OVERLOAD. TIME TO GET MOVING. LUKE! LET'S GO.

THANK YOU, HAN.

WAIT UNTIL WE'RE IN THE *FALCON*, A FEW LIGHT YEARS AWAY FROM HERE. THEN YOU CAN THANK ME IN STYLE, PRINCESS.

LUKE? WHERE IS THAT KID?

NO MATTER WHAT HAPPENS NEXT, I JUST WANT YOU TO KNOW, I APPRECIATE WHAT YOU'VE DONE HERE TODAY.

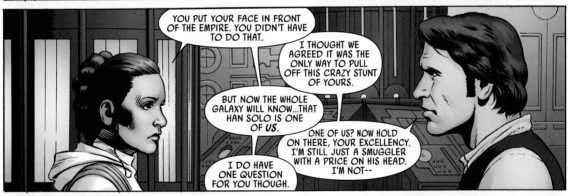

YOU PUT YOUR FACE IN FRONT OF THE EMPIRE. YOU DIDN'T HAVE TO DO THAT.

I THOUGHT WE AGREED IT WAS THE ONLY WAY TO PULL OFF THIS CRAZY STUNT OF YOURS.

BUT NOW THE WHOLE GALAXY WILL KNOW...THAT HAN SOLO IS ONE OF *US*.

ONE OF US? NOW HOLD ON THERE, YOUR EXCELLENCY. I'M STILL JUST A SMUGGLER WITH A PRICE ON HIS HEAD. I'M NOT--

I DO HAVE ONE QUESTION FOR YOU THOUGH.

WHY?

WHY WOULD YOU DO THAT?

WHAT IS IT YOU REALLY *WANT*, HAN SOLO?

UM...MAYBE NOW'S NOT REALLY THE BEST TIME TO...

WE READY TO GO?

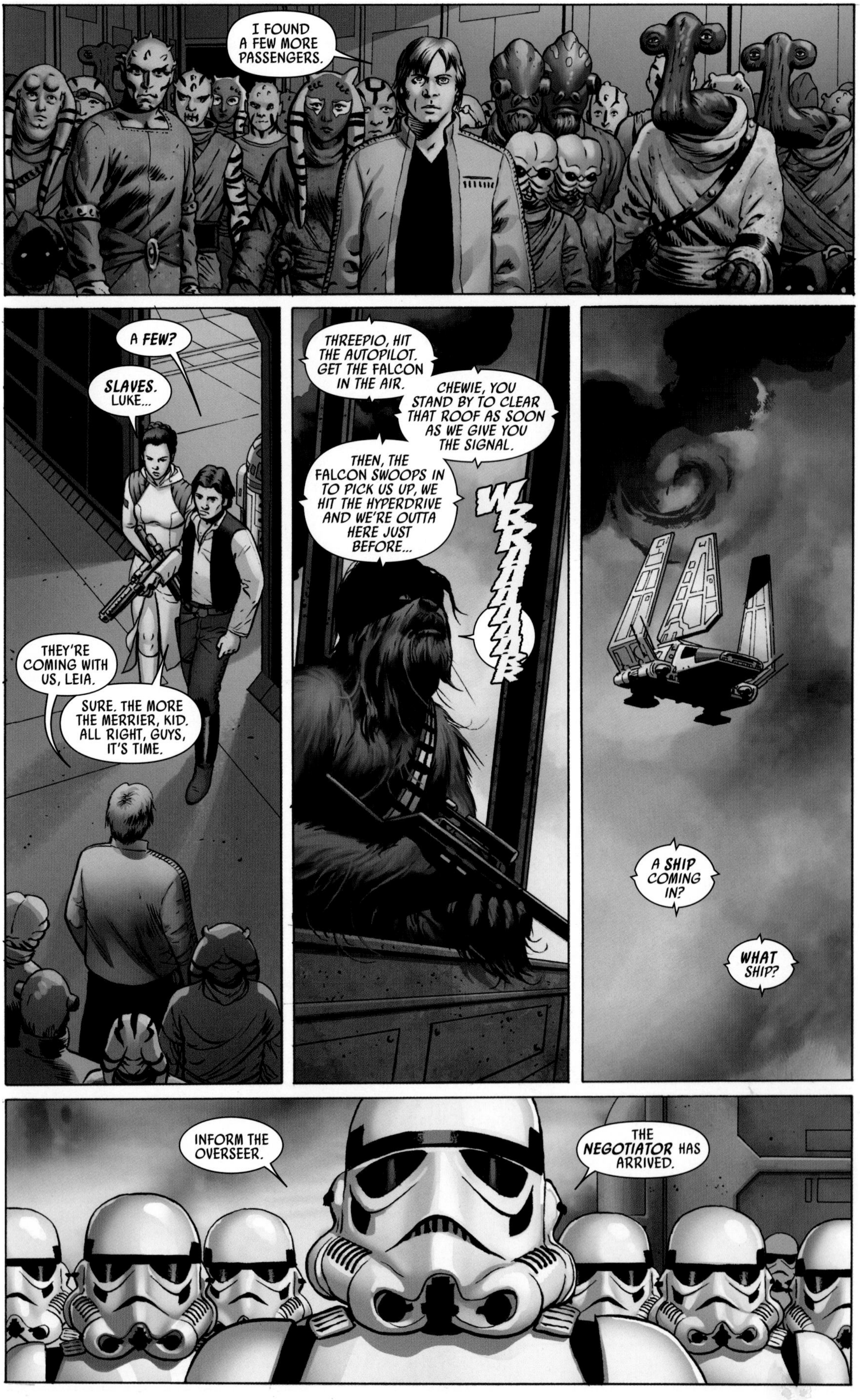
I FOUND A FEW MORE PASSENGERS.
A FEW?
SLAVES. LUKE...
THEY'RE COMING WITH US, LEIA.
SURE. THE MORE THE MERRIER, KID. ALL RIGHT, GUYS, IT'S TIME.
THREEPIO, HIT THE AUTOPILOT. GET THE FALCON IN THE AIR.
CHEWIE, YOU STAND BY TO CLEAR THAT ROOF AS SOON AS WE GIVE YOU THE SIGNAL.
THEN, THE FALCON SWOOPS IN TO PICK US UP, WE HIT THE HYPERDRIVE AND WE'RE OUTTA HERE JUST BEFORE...
WRAAAAAR
A SHIP COMING IN?
WHAT SHIP?
INFORM THE OVERSEER.
THE NEGOTIATOR HAS ARRIVED.

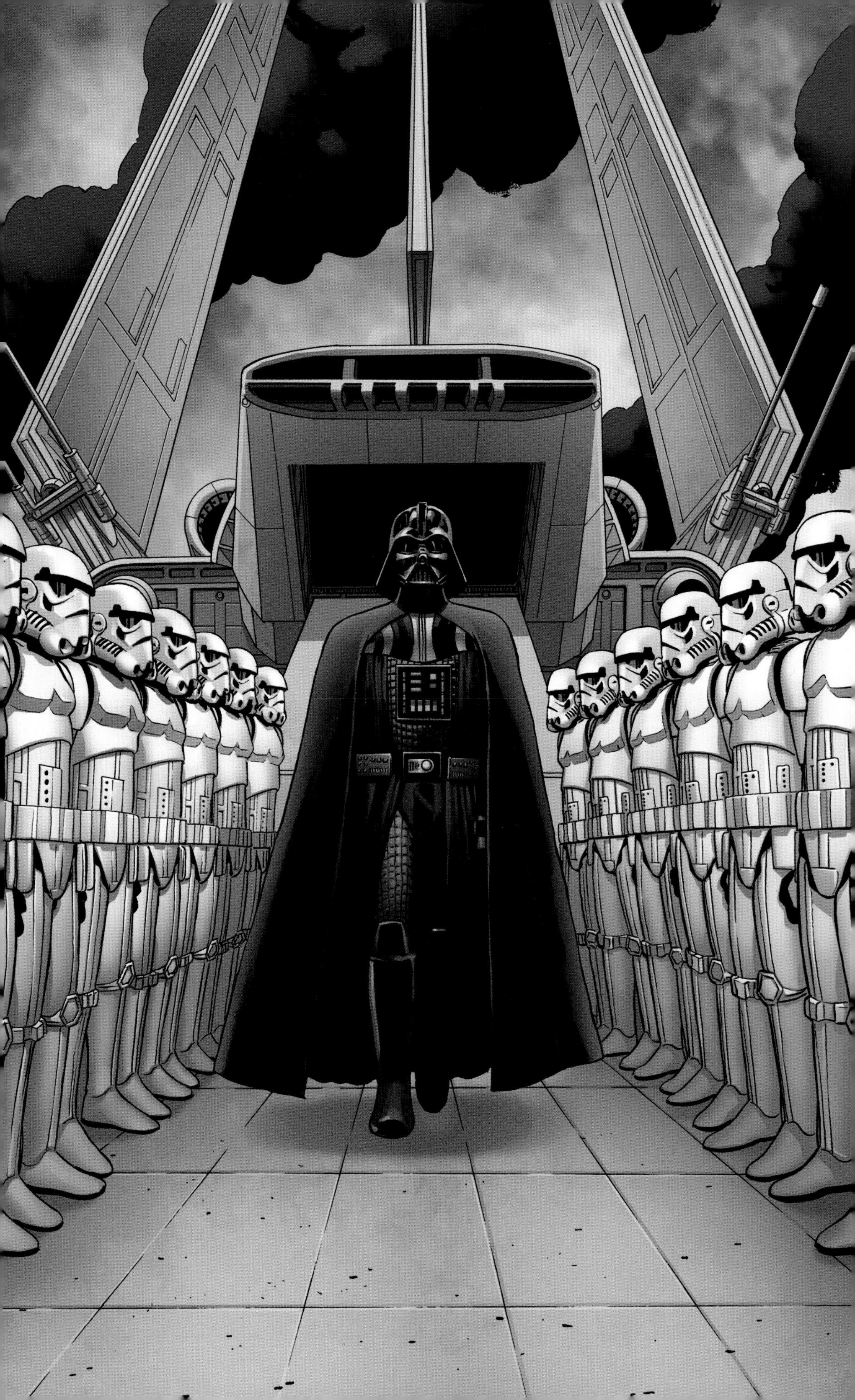

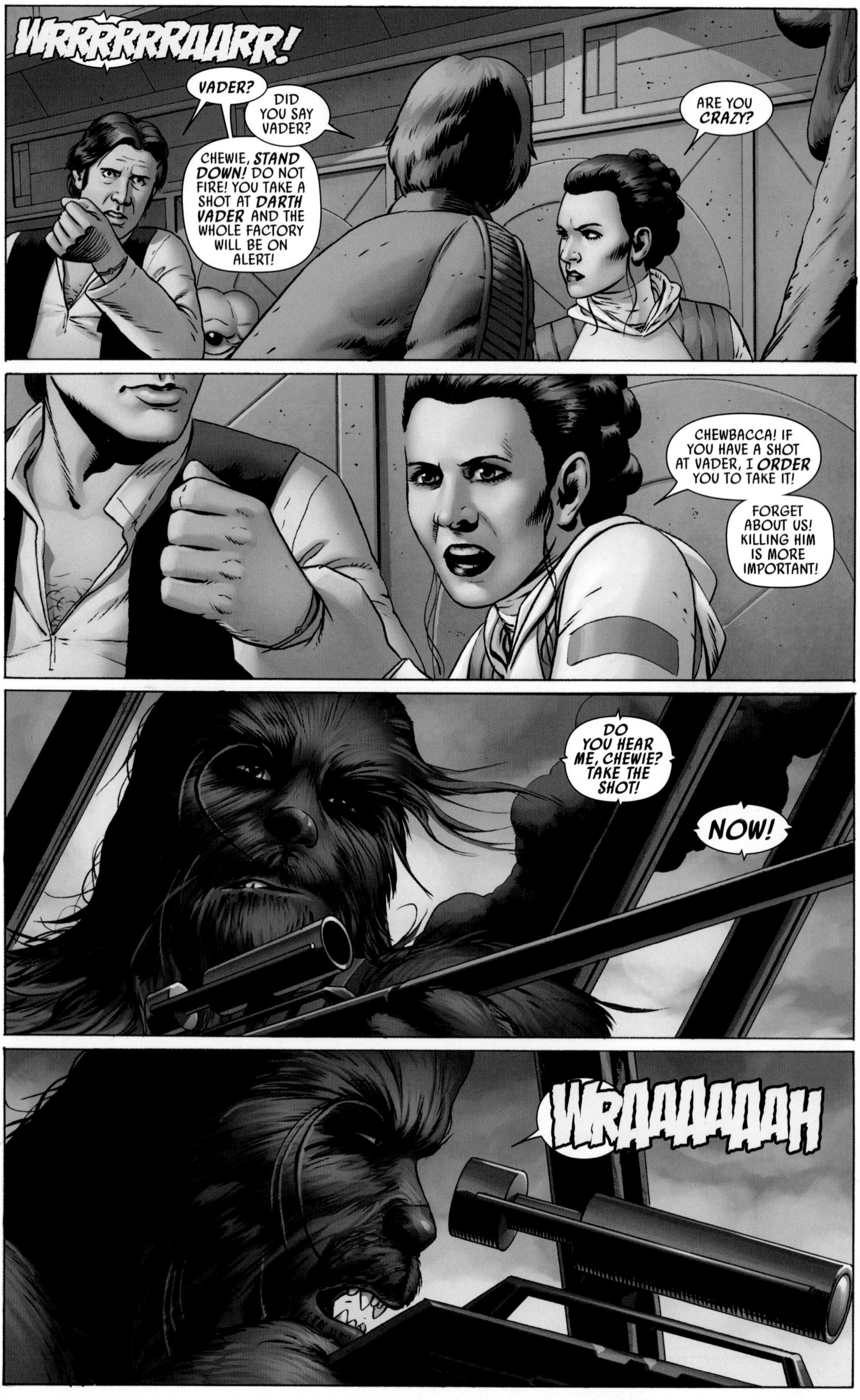
WRRRRRRRAARR!
VADER?
DID YOU SAY VADER?
ARE YOU CRAZY?
CHEWIE, STAND DOWN! DO NOT FIRE! YOU TAKE A SHOT AT DARTH VADER AND THE WHOLE FACTORY WILL BE ON ALERT!
CHEWBACCA! IF YOU HAVE A SHOT AT VADER, I ORDER YOU TO TAKE IT!
FORGET ABOUT US! KILLING HIM IS MORE IMPORTANT!
DO YOU HEAR ME, CHEWIE? TAKE THE SHOT!
NOW!
WRAAAAAAH

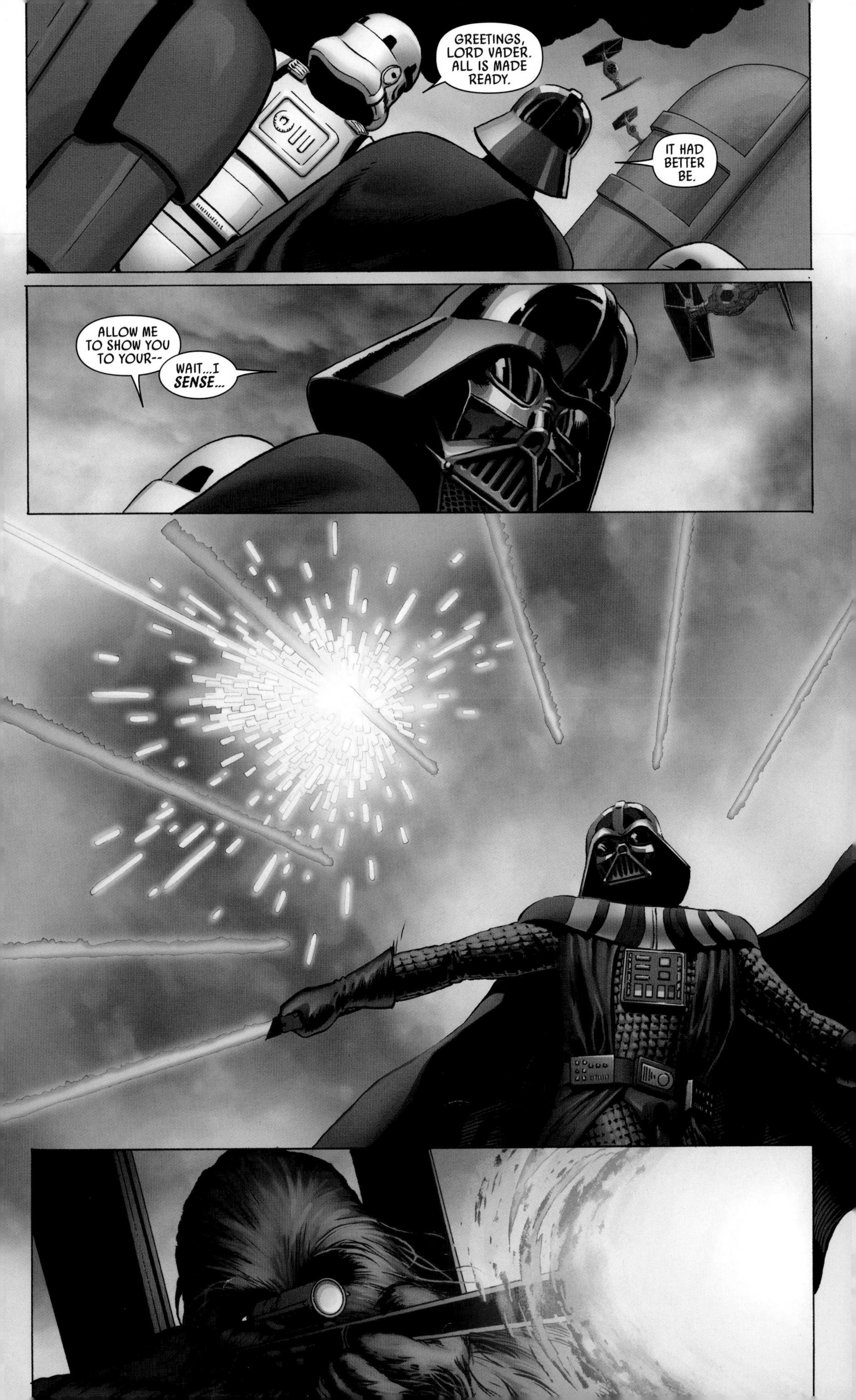
GREETINGS, LORD VADER. ALL IS MADE READY.
IT HAD BETTER BE.
ALLOW ME TO SHOW YOU TO YOUR--
WAIT...I SENSE...

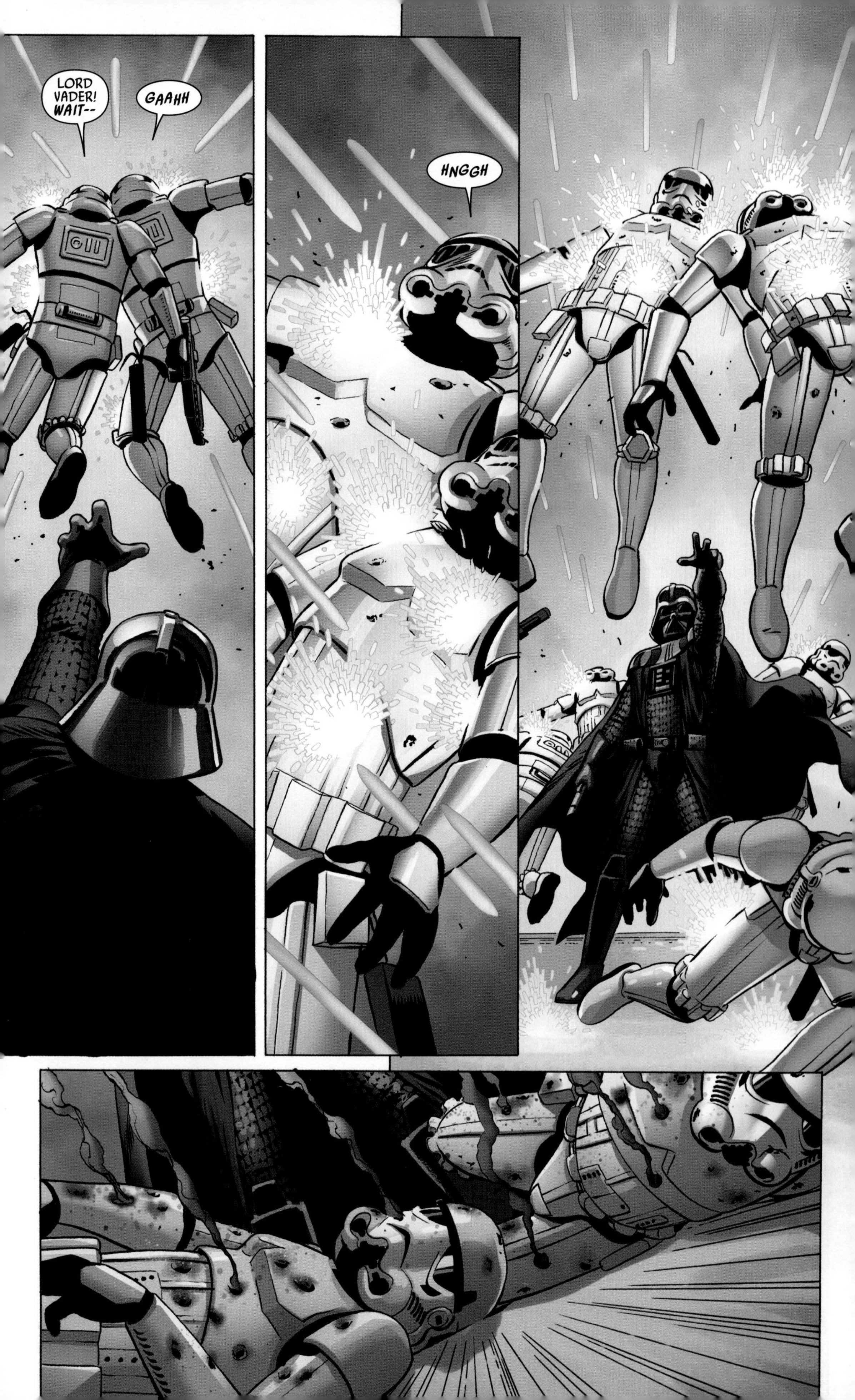
LORD VADER! WAIT--
GAAHH
HNGGH

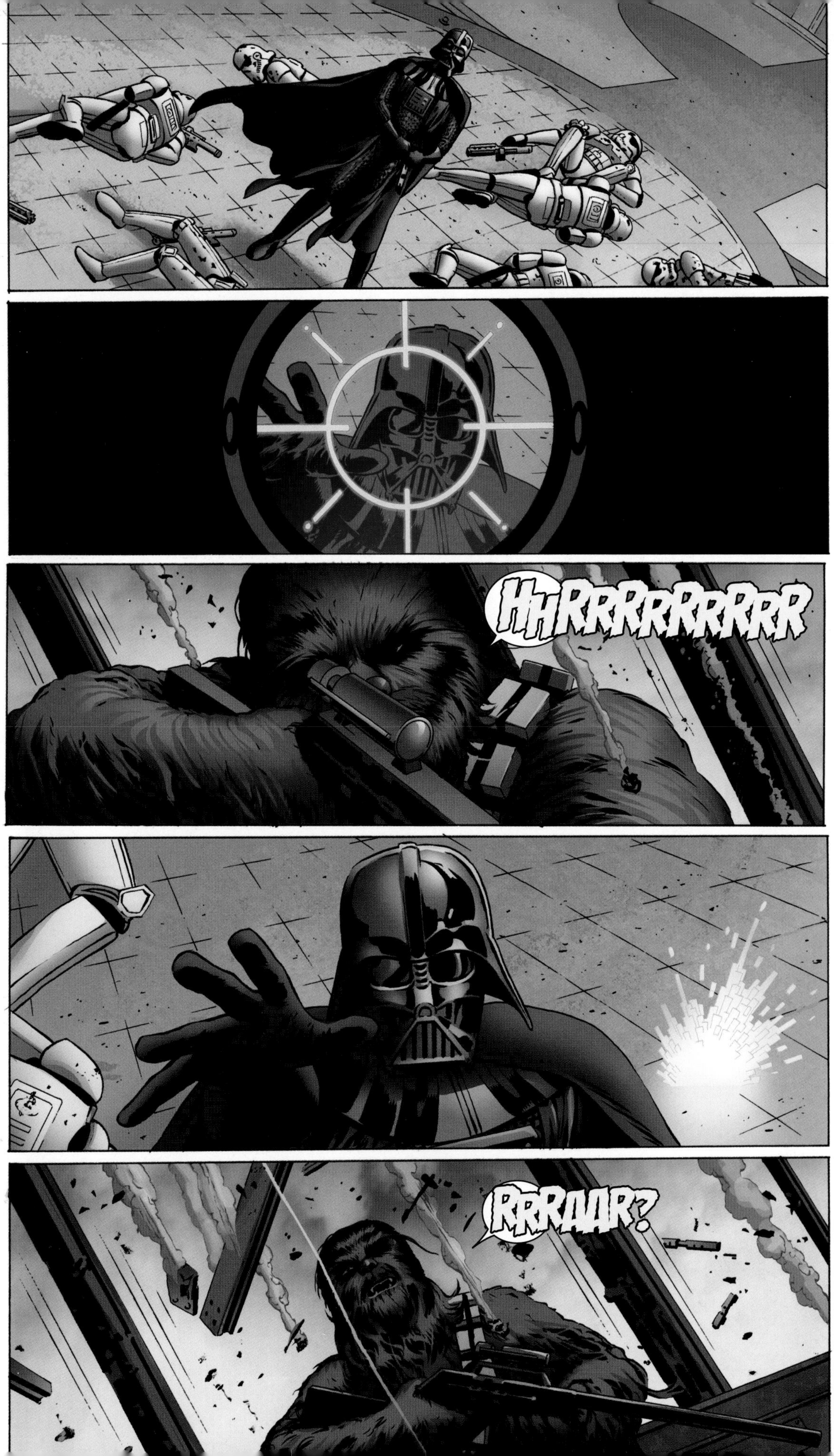
HHRRRRRRRRRR
RRRAAR?

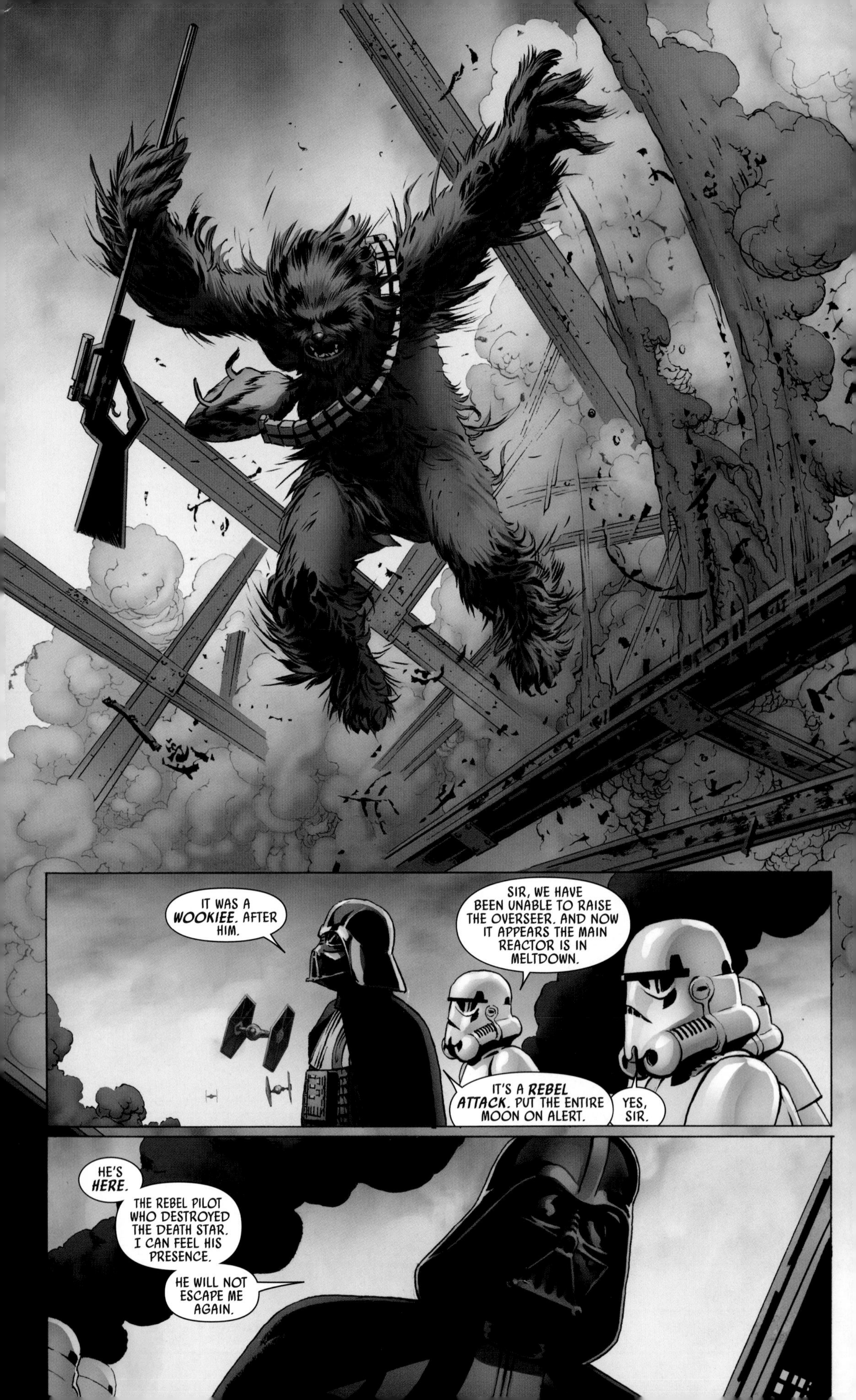
IT WAS A WOOKIEE. AFTER HIM.
SIR, WE HAVE BEEN UNABLE TO RAISE THE OVERSEER. AND NOW IT APPEARS THE MAIN REACTOR IS IN MELTDOWN.
IT'S A REBEL ATTACK. PUT THE ENTIRE MOON ON ALERT.
YES, SIR.
HE'S HERE.
THE REBEL PILOT WHO DESTROYED THE DEATH STAR. I CAN FEEL HIS PRESENCE.
HE WILL NOT ESCAPE ME AGAIN.

CHEWIE! CHEWIE, COME IN! WE'RE IN TROUBLE.

NO, NOT YET. WE CAN STILL--

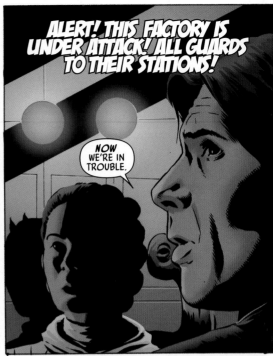

ALERT! THIS FACTORY IS UNDER ATTACK! ALL GUARDS TO THEIR STATIONS!

NOW WE'RE IN TROUBLE.

WE'LL HAVE TO BLAST OUR WAY OUT. WE STILL HAVE THE FALCON.

THREEPIO!

THREEPIO, GET US OUTTA HERE! HIT THE AUTO-PILOT!

I DID, SIR. I PRESSED THE BUTTON... FIVE MINUTES AGO.

I'M AFRAID... NOTHING HAPPENED.

YOU USELESS SACK OF SPRINGS! WHAT DID YOU DO TO MY SHIP?

OH, DEAR.

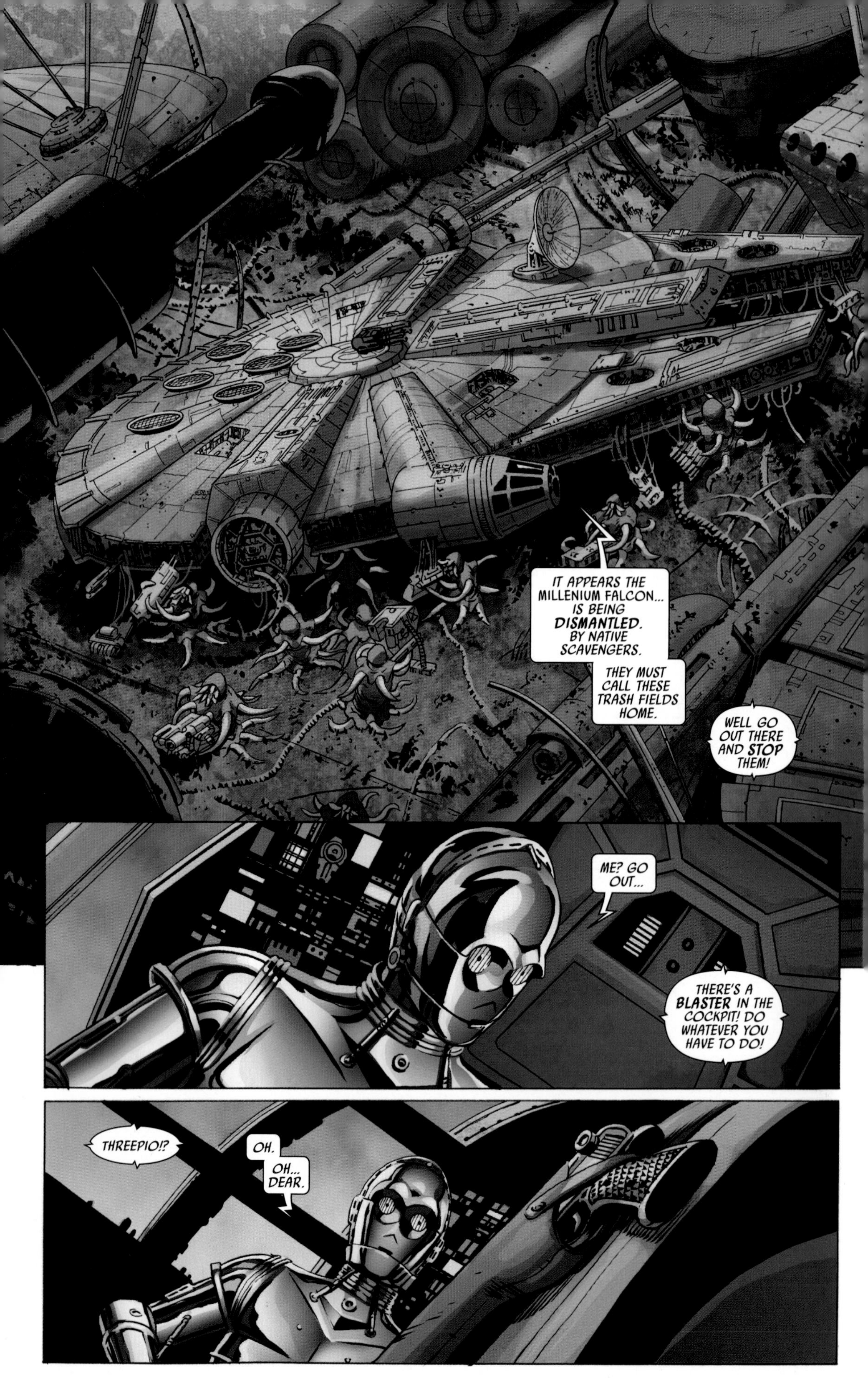

IT APPEARS THE MILLENIUM FALCON... IS BEING DISMANTLED. BY NATIVE SCAVENGERS.
THEY MUST CALL THESE TRASH FIELDS HOME.
WELL GO OUT THERE AND STOP THEM!
ME? GO OUT...
THERE'S A BLASTER IN THE COCKPIT! DO WHATEVER YOU HAVE TO DO!
THREEPIO!?
OH.
OH... DEAR.

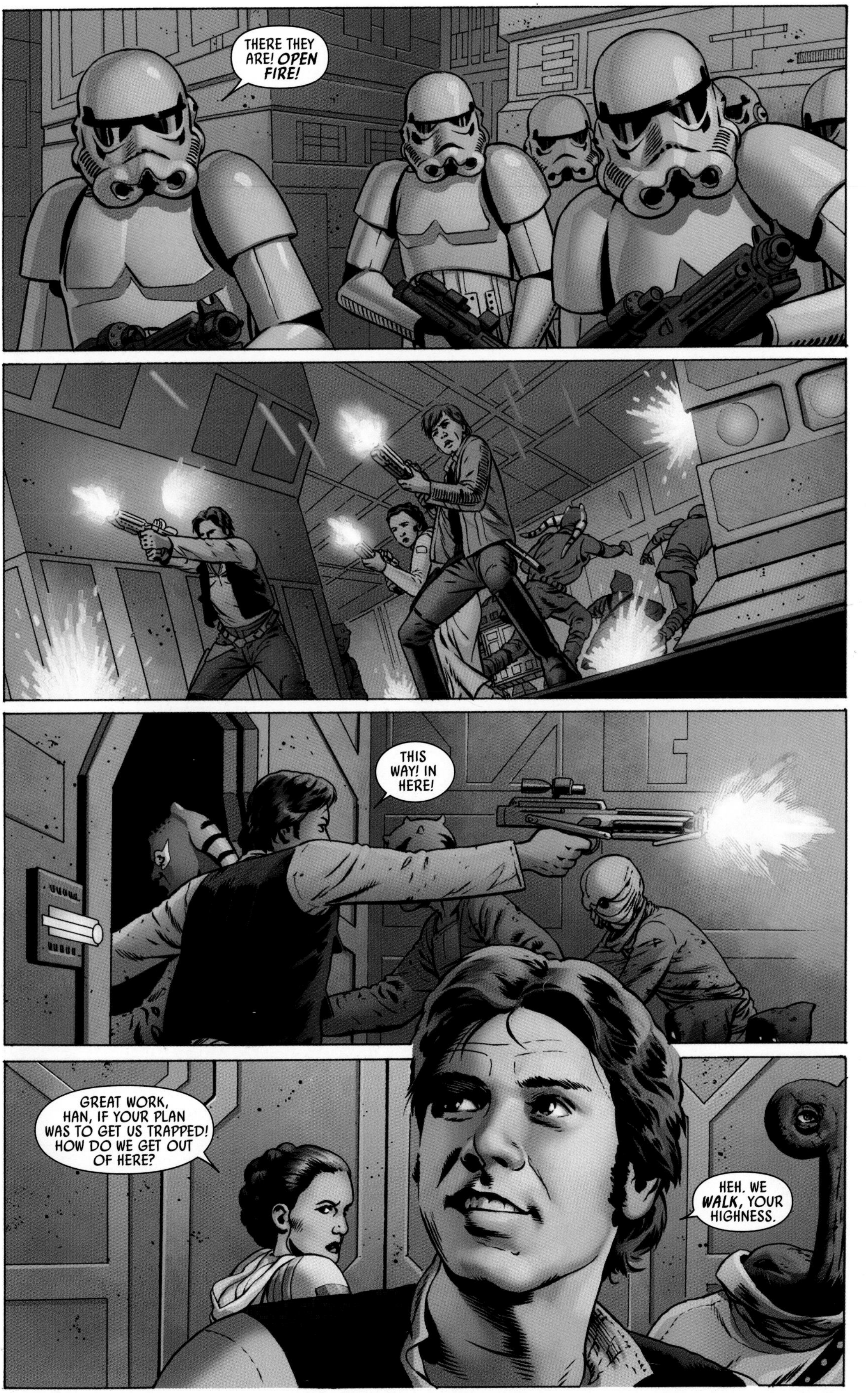
THERE THEY ARE! OPEN FIRE!
THIS WAY! IN HERE!
GREAT WORK, HAN, IF YOUR PLAN WAS TO GET US TRAPPED! HOW DO WE GET OUT OF HERE?
HEH. WE WALK, YOUR HIGHNESS.

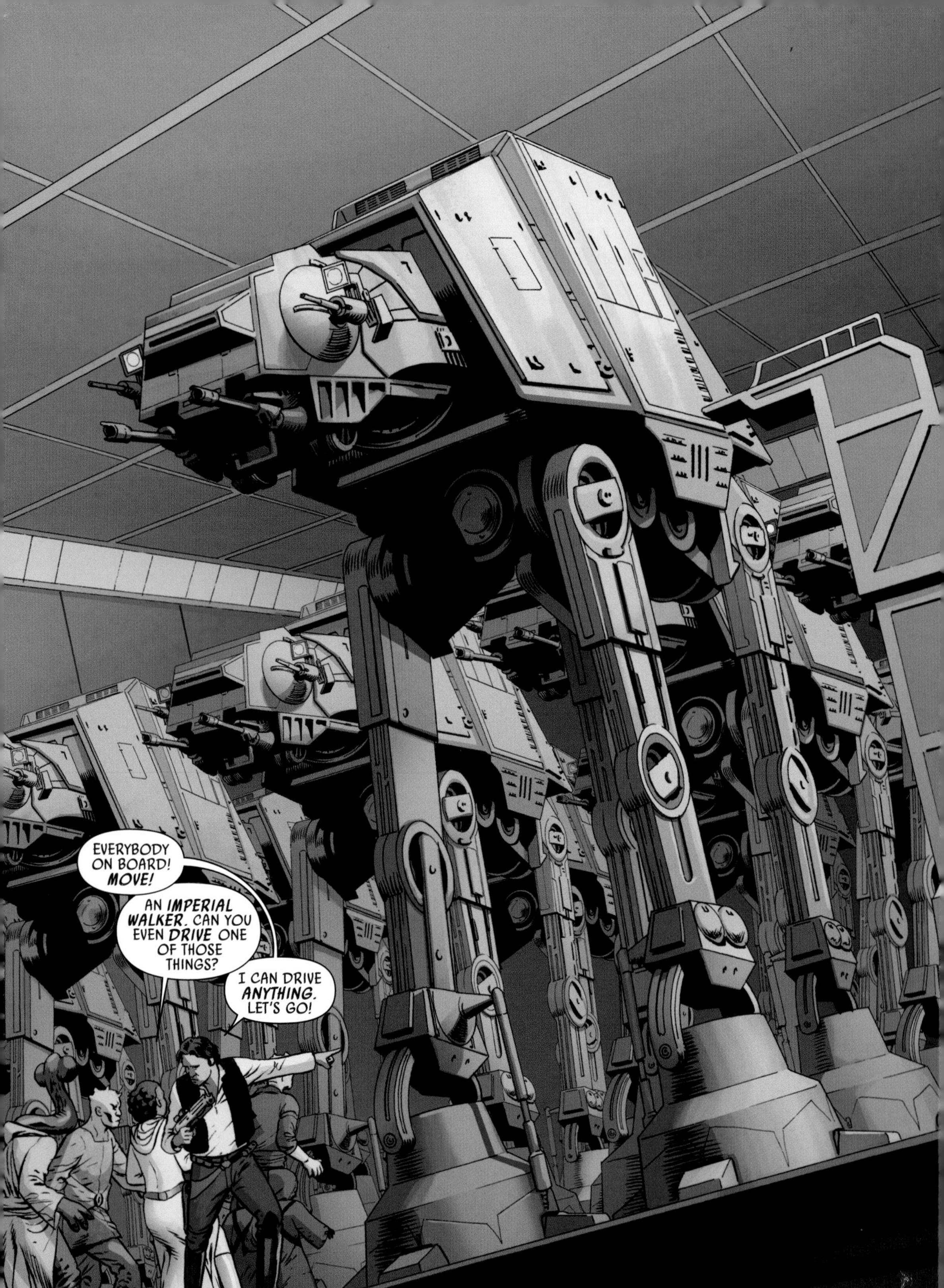
EVERYBODY ON BOARD! MOVE!
AN IMPERIAL WALKER. CAN YOU EVEN DRIVE ONE OF THOSE THINGS?
I CAN DRIVE ANYTHING. LET'S GO!

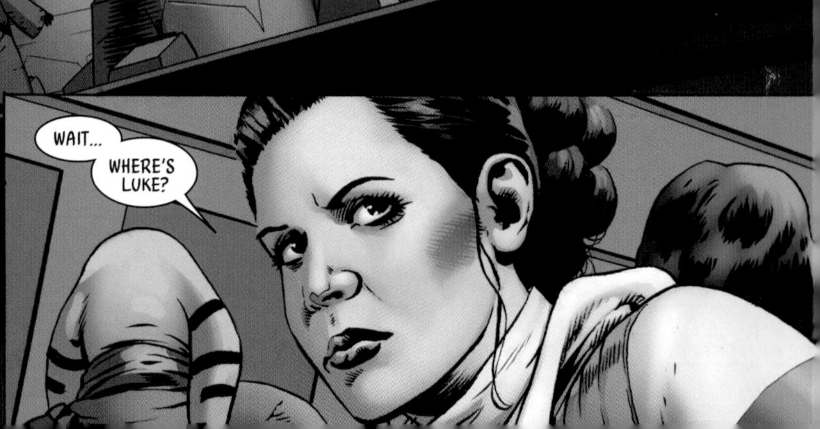
WAIT... WHERE'S LUKE?

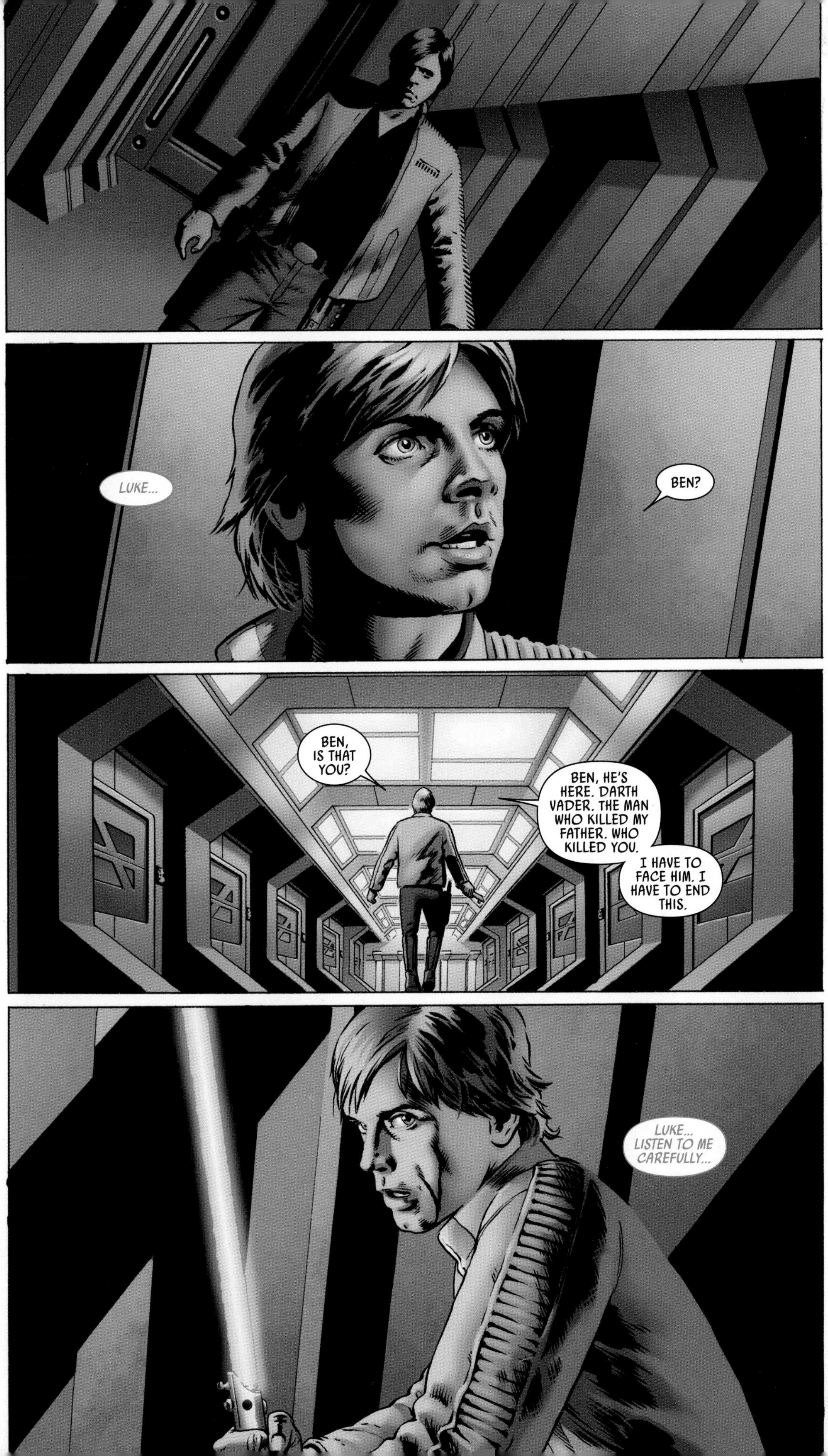
LUKE...
BEN?
BEN, IS THAT YOU?
BEN, HE'S HERE. DARTH VADER. THE MAN WHO KILLED MY FATHER. WHO KILLED YOU.
I HAVE TO FACE HIM. I HAVE TO END THIS.
LUKE... LISTEN TO ME CAREFULLY...

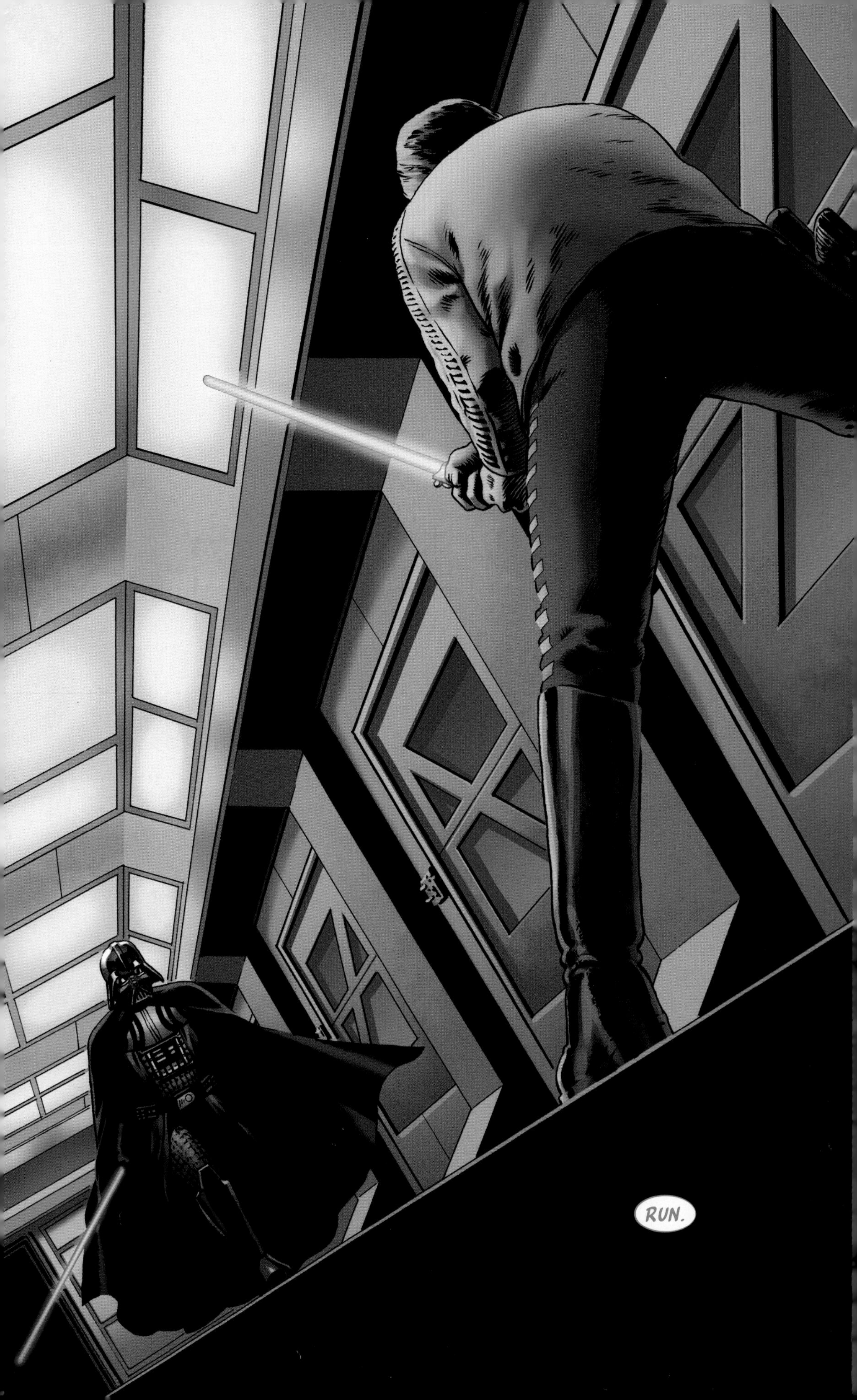
RUN.